**Two weeks.
Could he hang on for that long?**

He wasn't sure. He was about to say *No, thanks* when the image of Alisa popped into his head. The thought that she might give him an honest smile, more than her overly practiced, the-customer-is-right smile, gave him a jolt. He had no business thinking about that. Or wanting it.

He was definitely tired of being on the road. A clean room with a shower and free meals had a certain appeal.

Foolishly, he knew the real appeal was Alisa. He doubted she'd feel the same about him. Not if she knew the truth about how he'd spent the past three years. He didn't have to feel pressured to stay.

Slowly he stood. "Okay, I'll take your job."

**Books by Charlotte Carter**

Love Inspired

*Montana Hearts*
*Big Sky Reunion*
*Big Sky Family*
*Montana Love Letter*
*Home to Montana*

## *CHARLOTTE CARTER*

A multipublished author of more than fifty romances, cozy mysteries and inspirational titles, Charlotte Carter lives in Southern California with her husband of forty-nine years and their cat, Mittens. They have two married daughters and five grandchildren. When she's not writing, Charlotte does a little stand-up comedy, "G-Rated Humor for Grownups," and teaches workshops on the craft of writing.

# Home to Montana

## Charlotte Carter

Recycling programs for this product may not exist in your area.

™ LOVE INSPIRED BOOKS

ISBN-13: 978-0-373-81682-8

HOME TO MONTANA



This edition published by arrangement with Love Inspired Books.



www.LoveInspiredBooks.com

**Printed in U.S.A.**

Many nations will come and say,
Come, let us go up to the mountain of the Lord, to the temple of the God of Jacob. The law will go out from Zion, the word of the Lord from Jerusalem. He will judge between many peoples and will settle disputes for strong nations far and wide. They will beat their swords into plowshares and their spears into pruning hooks. Nation will not take up sword against nation, nor will they train for war anymore. Everyone will sit under their own vine and under their own fig tree, and no one will make them afraid, for the Lord Almighty has spoken.

—*Micah* 4:2–4

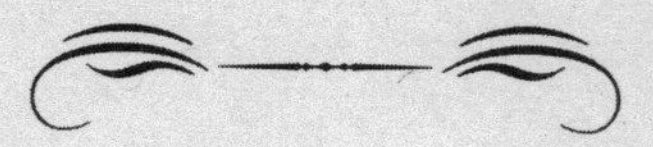

To all the men and women in uniform
who so bravely serve our country around the world,
and to those who wait for them at home,
you have our heartfelt thanks.

Special thanks to Kara Lennox and Mindy Neff;
you always make my books better.

# *Chapter One*

"A pretty lady like you shouldn't have to chop your own firewood."

Alisa Machak nearly sliced off her foot with the ax. She whirled toward the sound of the deep masculine voice.

The stranger stood in a column of sunlight that slid between the pine trees, highlighting his unkempt ebony hair, a matching beard and his equally disreputable dog sitting beside him. He wore old jeans and a khaki jacket that looked like it had come from an Army surplus store years ago.

A ripple of recognition stole through her, and a shiver raised the hair at her nape. *A drifter.*

Drifters passed through the town of Bear Lake, Montana, on a regular basis, some heading to Glacier National Park up Highway 93. Some with no particular destination in mind. None stayed long.

She'd learned that lesson ten years ago, a painful lesson she would not soon forget.

Flashing him the friendly smile she used with strangers, she hefted the ax. "Someone has to make kindling for the fire." She and her mother owned the Pine Tree Diner and the adjacent Pine Tree Inn. Unfortunately, their handyman, Jake Domino, had gone to stay with his daughter while she recovered from an auto accident. He'd be away at least a couple of weeks. So Alisa was chopping wood, among other chores that had to be done.

The stranger strolled toward her, all long legs and a gait that seemed a little uneven. "I'm pretty good with an ax. I'd be glad to help out. You wouldn't have to pay me."

She cocked her head in disbelief. This guy was a drifter with a silver tongue, the kind of man who Alisa had learned to keep at a distance while doing her smiling welcome-to-Pine-Tree-Diner shtick.

"If the diner has some scraps for Rags, I'd appreciate that." His baritone voice sounded as smooth and rich as homemade gravy.

That stopped her. "Rags?"

"My dog." He patted his thigh. The dog stood looking up at him waiting for his next command. "I figured when I found him that he looked like the old rag bag my mother used to have. She used the rags for cleaning and scrubbing the house."

"You found the dog?" She'd heard that some

pickup artists used a dog to put a woman at ease and get her off guard. Vulnerable. But surely a man like that wouldn't go out of his way to look so scruffy. Maybe his angle was playing for sympathy. She wasn't going to bite on that gimmick either.

"Found him a week or so ago. I pulled into a rest area to sleep. In Colorado, I think. Nobody else was around except Rags. No tags on him. No collar. And he was pretty hungry." Casually, he patted the dog's rough, ragamuffin coat colored in shades of wheat and tan. Floppy ears hung down on either side of an imposing head. "Guess you could say we sort of adopted each other."

He'd evidently been on the road a while. Just drifting, Alisa gathered. She supposed she ought to give him credit for taking care of a stray dog. The affection between the two seemed genuine. Two lost souls? Maybe. Or maybe not. Not that it was any of her business.

She looked toward the back of the diner, a building three stories tall, painted a bright pink, with family living quarters in the top two floors. Planter boxes filled with pots of colorful geraniums were placed in front of the second floor windows.

They'd have a big crowd tonight at the diner for their Thursday night special. Alisa had plenty of work to do inside, setting up for the evening while her mother, who everyone called Mama, handled the kitchen preparations. She really didn't have time to chop kindling for the big fire pit in the outdoor patio. September evenings had begun to turn cool.

She swung the ax, imbedding the blade in the chopping stump.

"Okay, mister…?"

"Nick. Nick Carbini."

"You've got yourself a deal, Nick. I'm Alisa Machak, half owner of the diner and motel next door. You make us a big pile of kindling, and I'll make sure your dog gets the best scraps in the county."

His dark beard shifted as he smiled, revealing a row of perfect white teeth. She noticed he had incredibly blue eyes, the color of the sky on a clear winter day. Squint lines fanned out at the corners.

Yet she also saw a hint of sadness in those clear eyes. A shadow of loneliness she sometimes saw in her own mirror and had learned to ignore.

She forced down her curiosity about where he had come from and why he had no place to go. That was none of her business either. From her perspective, he was simply another tourist passing through town.

"When you're done, stack the kindling under the lean-to by the kitchen. There's a wheelbarrow you can use." She gestured vaguely toward the woodpile.

"No problem. I've got it covered."

Based on his over six-foot height and the breadth of his shoulders, he'd be able to turn a whole cord of wood into kindling without breaking a sweat. At least that would save her from developing calluses on her palms for one day.

She turned, her steps light as she walked back to the kitchen entrance, her senses vividly aware of the *chunk, chunk* of the ax on a pine log. Aware of the stranger's strength. The power of his arms. His tempting smile.

And determined not to acknowledge how thoroughly he'd stirred memories she'd rather forget.

In the kitchen, three big pots of water steamed on the stove ready for Mama to drop in the loaves of bread dumplings for tonight's paprika chicken house special. A recipe Mama had learned from her own mother in Czechoslovakia.

Meanwhile, Hector Gomez, their short-order cook and kitchen helper was serving up buffalo burgers and fries and cold sandwiches for the midafternoon crowd.

The scent of baking bread, grilled meat and aromatic spices were as familiar to Alisa as a mother's perfume. She'd grown up here in the kitchen. First in a playpen safely away from spattering grease and well out from under the hurrying feet of the waitstaff. Later, standing on a chair so she could reach the prep tables, she'd rolled dough for biscuits and grated potatoes for potato pancakes, another Czech specialty. Served with apple sauce or sour cream, they had been a staple in Alisa's life.

Her father had done most of the cooking when Alisa was young while Mama worked the front of the diner. But he had passed away ten years ago, leaving Mama and Alisa to manage the diner.

This was her home, the place that held her heart and consumed the vast majority of her waking hours. The regular customers she served were her extended family. Old-timers who had lived here most of their lives. New folks who had more recently found a home under the wide Montana sky.

Mama turned and smiled. Her once blond hair was dulled now by streaks of gray. Her perpetual smile had formed permanent parentheses around her mouth.

"You finished making kindling already?"

Alisa shrugged out of her jacket and hung it on a coatrack near the door. "Nope. A drifter came by and offered to do it for me. All he asked in return was some scraps for his rather shaggy-looking dog."

"What? You didn't offer him a few dollars? A little supper?"

"He didn't ask." Everyone in town knew Mama

was a soft touch, although the locals rarely took advantage of her. Drifters weren't always so thoughtful. "I imagine he'll be hungry by the time he's through."

She washed up in a nearby sink, tied her hair back and went out front to see that they were ready for the evening rush.

Nick split another log, gratified by the growing pile of kindling by the stump. It felt good to use his muscles. He'd been cooped up in his pickup for too long. Driving and sleeping under the camper shell whenever and wherever he stopped.

Maybe he'd stay a few days in Bear Lake, camp somewhere nearby, hike the trails through the forest, check out the house where he'd been born. The house where his mother had died some twenty years ago.

His throat tightened on the memory of his mother so sick she couldn't get out of bed. So pale it was like all of the blood had been sucked out of her. He'd only been ten years old when the ambulance came to take her away forever.

Not long after that his dad had piled their few possessions in his old, beat-up truck. They'd gone east and south, moving a dozen times whenever his dad lost his job or got restless. Finally, when Nick had managed to get a high school diploma he'd bailed on his father and joined the army.

He'd been out now for nearly four years.

A couple of weeks ago he'd tried to reconnect with his dad. His father had tossed him out of his house in Baton Rouge, or more accurately his dad's current girlfriend had insisted he leave. She didn't want an ex-con living in her house. Nick's old man hadn't ever been much of a father so he sided with the girlfriend, who doubled as his drinking buddy and sometimes, Nick suspected, his punching bag.

Nick hadn't had a destination in mind when he left Baton Rouge. He'd simply gotten in his truck and headed north.

But the farther north he drove, the more the thought of Bear Lake drew him. He couldn't tell if it was God who was leading him or his own childhood memories of home. Maybe both.

He swung the ax again. Two pieces of kindling jumped from the stump onto the ground. He paused long enough to take off his jacket and look around. Sweat edged down his spine.

Nice layout Ms. Alisa Machak had here. A good business. Even in the middle of the afternoon there were a fair number of cars parked out front. He hadn't lied about her being a pretty lady, either. Hair a honey blond that skimmed her shoulders. Shoulders much too slender to wield an ax with so much strength. Or maybe she was working on a heap of determination more than sheer muscle power.

Nice eyes, too. A dark blue like the deepest part of a lake. But she hadn't smiled much, not at him. He didn't blame her for that. He must look pretty rough after a couple of weeks on the road.

Rags came trotting back from wherever he'd been with a stick in his mouth.

"You'd better stay close by, buddy. If you hang around, you're gonna get some really tasty scraps. That pretty lady promised you'd get the best in the county."

Tilting his head, Rags looked up at Nick with his big, brown eyes and whined. Trying to sucker Nick into throwing the stick.

"No, I can't play now. Gotta turn all this split wood into kindling. Maybe later, huh?"

Nick hung his jacket over a tree limb and got back to work. Three more whacks, and another split log became kindling.

"Hey, mister. Is that your dog?"

Rags stood and stretched, the branch still in his mouth.

Nick rested the ax head on the stump. A blond kid with a head full of cowlicks and a backpack slung over his shoulder stood a few feet from him. He looked to be about nine or ten.

"Mine 'til he decides otherwise," Nick said.

"Is he friendly?"

"Friendly enough. You want to pet him?"

The boy ditched his backpack on the ground and

rushed forward, dropping to his knees. “Does he have a name?”

“I call him Rags.”

“Hiya, Rags.” Cautiously, he petted the dog’s neck and back.

Rags’s tail began an upbeat tempo that wobbled his whole rear end.

“Does he like to play fetch?”

“Give it try. See what happens.” Nick knew from experience that Rags could wear out a man’s arm before he’d quit fetching any old stick.

He watched with amusement as the boy gently took the branch from Rags. Alert, Rags was already into the game when the boy tossed the stick a few feet away. Rags had it back to the youngster in milliseconds and lay down waiting for the next go around. His tail semaphored his readiness.

“You might want to toss it a little farther,” Nick suggested mildly.

The youngster shot it toward a wooded area, and soon boy and dog were running around full blast. Laughter and barking filled the clearing where Nick wrestled split logs onto the stump.

In that moment, an emotion so powerful he almost dropped the ax rose up in Nick. A sensation of loneliness so stark and desperate he had to close his eyes. He wanted to run away. To forget the past. Start over.

But that wasn’t possible.

* * *

Alisa heard the ruckus outside and stepped to the kitchen door. Her breath caught in her lungs when she saw her son playing with the stranger's dog.

*No! Don't get attached to the dog. The drifter will take him away. That's what drifters do. They leave.*

"Greg! It's time to come in." Panic raised her voice to a shrill note.

"But Mom, I'm playing with Rags now."

"Now, Greg. Come get a snack and start your homework."

"Just two more minutes."

Alisa took a step out onto the porch toward her son, planted her fists on her hips. "One, two..."

Greg's shoulders slumped. He tossed the stick he'd been playing with aside and trudged toward the house while the dog looked on with the stick once again in his mouth.

Her heart broke for her little boy, but in this case she knew she was right. She had to protect her son from smooth talking men who broke promises and left plenty of heartache behind.

She only wished she'd known that ten years ago.

After Greg washed up, Alisa shooed him over to the last stool at the counter out front in the diner. She brought him a bowl of fresh-picked wild blackberries and a slice of toast spread with peanut butter.

"How was school today?"

"Okay, I guess."

"Anything exciting happen?"

"Pete Muldoon had to go to the principal's office again."

"Why this time?" Poor little Pete seemed to be perpetually in trouble.

Greg took a big bite of toast, chewing while he spoke. "We were playing tag at recess. He was *it* and followed Tammy into the girls bathroom to catch her."

Alisa suppressed a grin. "Oh, dear."

"Tammy wasn't mad or anything. I think she likes Pete."

But maybe not so much in the restroom. "You do your homework after you finish your snack. If you need help, let me know."

"'Kay." He spooned a blackberry into his mouth. Juice dribbled out around the corners. "Mom, could we maybe have a dog someday?"

She and her son had had this conversation any number of times. "I can't have a dog inside the diner, honey. You know that. And there are too many wild animals around to leave a dog outside all the time."

"We could keep him upstairs with us."

Reaching across the table, she pulled her son's

head toward her, kissing him on the crown. "Sorry, munchkin. No dogs for us."

Dogs were for families with a mother and father and two-point-five children who lived in houses with white picket fences. Not for single moms who worked double shifts and often smelled like grilled hamburger meat at the end of the day.

Nick stacked the last of the kindling under the lean-to and grabbed his jacket.

"Come on, Rags. Let's see what kind of table scraps Ms. Alisa has come up with." Maybe there'd be a few scraps suitable for a hungry man too, he mused, his stomach growling.

He knocked once on the kitchen door but stopped when he heard a woman inside yelling. Not Alisa's voice. Someone older. And far angrier.

"What you mean, you can't come 'til tomorrow? We got two hundred people coming tonight. I'm not going to—" After a moment of silence, the woman ran off a string of words that Nick couldn't understand but guessed were an expression of her frustration.

He took a step back from the kitchen door. "I think we ought to wait a while for those scraps, buddy." But before he could get away, the door flew open.

An older woman, her cheeks flushed with anger

appeared, her eyes burning with fury. "What do you want?"

"It's okay, ma'am. Just wanted you to know the kindling—"

"You know anything about fixing a dishwasher?"

The abrupt question stopped him. He blinked. Beyond the woman he could see the shine of stainless steel prep tables and refrigerators. He caught the scent of garlic, onions and paprika. Heard the clatter of pans and sizzle of meat on a grill.

Sweat formed on his brow and dripped down his neck. His breathing became labored.

Automatically, he dug his hand into his pocket and began to rhythmically squeeze the rubber ball the prison chaplain had given him. It was supposed to relax and distract him. *Don't lose it. There's nothing to be afraid of. Think of something else. They're only memories. It isn't happening now.*

"Mister, I've got a busted dishwasher that's full of dirty dishes. If I don't get it fixed in a hurry, we're going to be hand washing every single dish in the place. Now…" She put her fist on her hip in much the same way as Alisa had earlier. "You know anything about fixing machines or don't you?"

"I, ah…" He did have some idea. And he sympathized with the woman's problem. But fixing the dishwasher would mean going inside the kitchen. Being surrounded by reflections that flashed and sparked off the stainless steel equipment, bringing back memories he struggled to forget. Images he couldn't ignore. Afghanistan. An attack on his outpost. A shiny kitchen turned into a bloodbath. His crew dead or dying.

He clenched his teeth. Squeezed the ball harder. *Don't think about it.*

Alisa, the blonde who'd been chopping kindling slipped up behind the older woman. "What's going on, Mama?"

"The dishwasher is busted. I called Samson. He can't come 'til tomorrow."

A frown etched Alisa's forehead, matching her mother's. "Guess we'll just have to make-do somehow."

Helplessly, Mama threw up her hands. "It must be God's will."

"I can try to fix it." Nick didn't know why he'd spoken. Maybe it was the mention of God. Or the thought that the Lord had brought him here for a reason. *To fix a dishwasher?* He nearly choked on how ridiculous that sounded.

Mother and daughter both gaped at him.

"You know how to fix a dishwasher?" Doubt deepened the grooves in Alisa's forehead.

"I've fixed a few. No guarantees."

"Come on inside, young man." Mama opened the door wider. "Give it a try. We've got nothing to lose."

He signaled Rags to stay. Using every ounce of courage he had, Nick crossed the threshold into the shining bright world of a commercial kitchen.

Blackness oozed in around the corners of his mind. The scream of bullets and crying men assaulted his ears. He fought to keep them at bay.

This was the world that had once been his to command. A place where he'd felt at home as the top chef.

After Afghanistan, would that ever be true again?

# *Chapter Two*

Nick gritted his teeth.

He could do this. All he had to do was keep focused on the present. The mission. Find the dishwasher. Figure out what was wrong. And fix it. Plus keep his eyes averted from shiny surfaces that inevitably awakened horrific memories.

He forced himself to remember his mother's kitchen. The smell of oregano and tomato sauce simmering on the stove. The laughter they'd shared when she taught him how to make fresh pasta. The good times before she got sick.

Alisa's mother marched ahead of him. He watched her feet, her black leather granny shoes treading on the spotless, blue-gray, antiskid tile floor. A well-kept kitchen. A-rated and ready to pass muster with the toughest health inspector.

She stopped so abruptly, Nick almost ran into her.

"This is the creature that has decided to plague

me." She slapped her palm on the side of the upright stainless steel dishwasher. Clearly an older model, probably prone to problems.

Nick used the sleeve of his jacket to wipe the sweat from his brow and squinted to minimize reflections. "What's wrong with it?"

"She won't start. Hector, he pushes the button. Nothing happens." She thumbed toward the fry cook working at his station, a small guy who looked young enough to be a new enlistee. "I push the button. Nothing happens." The rhythm of her voice spoke of foreign roots.

The washer not starting meant the problem could be anything from being unplugged to a motor that had burned out.

Frowning, he looked along the back of the machine. "Do you have a flashlight?"

Almost instantly, Alisa thrust a heavy-duty flashlight toward him. "Here. I thought you might need one. We lose power pretty often in the winter so we've got these positioned all around the diner. Summer lightning storms can knock out the power too."

Their eyes met as he took the flashlight from her hand. The depth of her blue eyes and her furrowed frown told him she was dubious he could fix anything. He wasn't all that confident either.

He checked behind the machine, handed her back the flashlight and grabbed hold of the dishwasher. “I need to move it out from the wall a few inches so I can get a better look.”

“It’s heavy,” she warned.

“Yeah, I figured that.” Rocking it side-to-side, he inched the dishwasher far enough forward to get a better look but not so far that he’d mess with the drain or water hoses.

He took the flashlight again and squeezed up against the wall. The machine was plugged into a power strip along with neighboring equipment. While he couldn’t reach the plug, he had no reason to think it wasn’t providing power. Everything else was working.

He fussed with the connection at the back of the machine. It seemed solid.

“You’re sure you know what you’re doing?” Alisa asked.

He glanced over his shoulder. With her blond hair pulled back, she looked younger than she had outside. No blemish marred her fair complexion. “I’ve eliminated the two most obvious reasons it won’t work. Your mother’s electrician would’ve charged her a hundred bucks for doing that. I’m saving her money.”

“Very thoughtful of you.”

“I’m that kind of guy.”

“Glad to hear it.” Her overly friendly smile didn’t quite reach her eyes.

He sensed her distrust and turned back to the

machine, opening the door. Racks of dirty dishes were stacked inside. He pressed the latch on the door.

"Try starting it now," he requested.

"The door has to be closed before it will start."

"Unless the latch is the problem."

"Okay," she said, still dubious. She punched the start button. The motor hummed and water spewed onto the dirty dishes.

Nick shut the door and the action came to a stop. He grinned. *Good guess, Carbini!*

"How did you do that?" Alisa asked, her eyes wide with surprise.

Mama scurried across the kitchen. "You got it fixed already?"

"Not yet, ma'am." He opened the door again. "Looks like I'm going to need a screwdriver." Fortunately, the only problem was that the latch had loosened and didn't make a solid electrical contact. Thus the machine wouldn't work. It wasn't the first time Nick had seen that particular problem. The heavy use of equipment in a 24-7 military kitchen meant lots of parts broke. He'd had to learn to keep things going with whatever he could find.

From somewhere Alisa produced a screwdriver. With a few twists, Nick tightened down the latch.

He closed the door and stepped back. "Okay, try it again."

The motor hummed. The water whooshed.

Mrs. Machak threw her arms around Nick and kissed both of his cheeks. "You're a genius! Thank you! Thank you!" She patted his face, which was now hot with embarrassment.

"It wasn't that hard to do, ma'am."

"You call me Mama. Everyone does. I'm going to bring you a big plate of my special chicken and dumplings. Alisa will show you a nice place to sit out front—"

"I really can't—" He figured he looked a mess, his face streaked with sweat from fighting the memories that were reflected in the stainless steel. Even without that, he was pretty dirty from chopping wood and being on the road so long. "My dog's outside. I was hoping he'd get some table scraps." He glanced at Alisa.

She nodded. "I'll fix Rags a dish."

"Thanks. And if you don't mind, Mama. I appreciate your offer of supper, but I'd just as soon eat on the porch with my dog. Looking the way I do, I think I'd scare off your customers if I ate out front." Being outside would also get him away from the reflections. Give him some space to breathe again.

Mama narrowed her eyes, appraising him. "Trust me, we've seen worse. But if that's what you'd like, it's fine with me."

He made his way out the back door and walked halfway into the yard, his leg more painful than usual, before he could draw a comfortable breath of cool, fresh air. He supposed the prison chaplain who counseled him about his post-traumatic stress disorder would say it was a good thing he'd done. He'd gone into a kitchen without having a full panic attack like the one he'd had when they'd assigned him to prison kitchen duty. They'd transferred his work detail to the prison laundry in a hurry.

Good thing or not, he was still shaking on the inside.

Rags did a couple of circles around Nick. He knelt and wrapped his arms around the dog. A calming sensation eased his nerves. The tight muscles of his neck and shoulders relaxed. More than one night since he'd found Rags, the dog had awakened Nick before his recurring nightmare had a chance to send him screaming out into the cold. Instead, he'd buried his face in the dog's fur, holding on while the bloody images faded.

"Your dinner's on the way, buddy." His voice was hoarse, his mouth dry. "Sorry it took me so long."

The back door opened. Alisa stood backlighted on the porch with two plates in her hands, her slender figure revealed in silhouette.

He pushed up to his feet.

"You really could eat inside," she said. "We get

hikers and fishermen who've been out in the wilderness for weeks that look worse than you do."

"I'm fine here, thanks." He took Rags' plate and put it down at the foot of the steps. "Here you go, buddy." Tomorrow he'd have to find a grocery store and stock up on dog food. He didn't usually take handouts, but he had to admit the paprika smell of the chicken was enough to make his mouth water. Rags didn't have any objection to the chunks of steak on his plate, either.

"We do appreciate you fixing the dishwasher. I was afraid Mama was going to blow a gasket if we had to do without until our electrician could get here tomorrow."

"Glad I could help."

Alisa hesitated for a moment before handing him the plate of chicken. "Just bring your dirty plates inside when you're done."

He nodded and watched her walk back into the kitchen. An ache of loneliness rose inside him, and he wished he could follow her into her world. A world that used to be his.

He'd be a fool on any number of levels if he acted on that impulse. She'd be worse than a fool if she let him.

He bent over his plate, said a silent grace and dug into the chicken. The mixture of sour cream, paprika and garlic in the sauce slid across his tongue giving his taste buds a treat. He chewed the fork-tender chicken thoughtfully.

Mama Machak sure knew how to cook.

Alisa shook her head as she returned to the kitchen.

The man was a puzzle. Scruffy and unkempt, a drifter but well-spoken. A man who worried about his dog before eating his own supper.

Normally she'd find that admirable.

In this case, she'd put it down to her quixotic quirk that made her a sucker for the underdog.

"You get that young man his dinner?" Mama plated two chicken specials and added a serving of steamed julienne vegetables.

"He's eating on the porch with his dog. Just like he wanted."

"He's a good man. I can tell."

"Why? Because he fixed a switch on our dishwasher?" If she'd known what was wrong, she could have fixed it herself.

"No, it's in his eyes. They're honest eyes."

Alisa thought they were intense eyes. Penetrating. Almost mesmerizing. She didn't know about honest. And wasn't about to volunteer to test Mama's intuition.

"You think he's looking for a job?" Mama asked.

"I doubt he'll stay around that long."

Mama slid the two plated dinners under the

heat lamp where the waitress could pick them up. "What's his name?"

"Nick. Carboni? Caloni? Something like that."

Cocking her head, Mama frowned. "There used to be a family here. Carbini, I think it was. The mother was sickly all the time. The father worked summers at the mill and got drunk all winter. There was a cute little boy—"

Alisa gasped. "Nick Carbini! I remember him from third grade. He had a neat smile and told knock knock jokes and dumb riddles until we were all sick of them. But he couldn't be the same—" This Nick rarely smiled. She doubted he was into telling jokes. There was too much sadness about him. Still, as she remembered her classmate's eyes…

"When the mother died, the old man took the boy off with him," Mama related. "I wondered sometimes if the youngster would be all right with his father. He wasn't a good example for the boy." She tossed two New York strip steaks on the grill, and they sizzled.

"Maybe," Mama mused, "your young man has come home to stay."

"He's not my young anything."

Mama pulled off her disposable gloves and tossed them in a nearby trash container. "You watch the steaks, sweetie. I'm going see if young Mr. Carbini would like a job."

"Mama! What kind of a job? You don't know anything about the man. He could be a criminal for all you know. Just because you knew him as a boy and felt sorry for him, doesn't mean you can trust him as a man. It doesn't sound like he came from a very good family."

"Not everyone is as lucky as you were to have a nice mama and papa. From what I've seen, Nick Carbini knows enough to fill in for Jake for a couple of weeks."

Mama grabbed her sweater from the coatrack, tossed it around her shoulders and stepped out onto the porch.

Alisa rolled her eyes. Nick might have had a rough life, but he was still a drifter. She didn't want him or his dog around, not when Greg was so obviously drawn to the pair. Not when she knew her own weakness.

If Nick decided he'd take the job, she'd have to make sure to keep her distance.

How she'd manage to do that with him working around the diner was beyond her.

Nick looked up as Mama stepped out onto the porch. At the same time, Rags lifted his head and his tail began to swipe through the air. Greedy as he was, he was probably hoping for another plate of scraps.

"This chicken is great. Wonderful flavor," Nick said. "I've never had dumplings like these either."

Mama beamed. "My mama taught me. It's a Czechoslovakian dish. Some people use water for the dumplings, but milk is better."

"Gives it more flavor and body."

"Yes, absolutely." She sat down on the step beside Nick. "So, young man, are you looking for a job?"

Petting Rags, he frowned. "I don't plan to hang around long." He had no idea where he might go next. But he would leave as soon as his flashbacks returned. The nightmares that woke him in a cold sweat. Then he'd move on. Trying to outrun them.

So far that hadn't worked.

"How 'bout for two weeks? Our handyman's gone," Mama said. "Jake's daughter was hurt real bad in an accident in Spokane. He plans to come back when she's able to manage on her own."

Two weeks. Could he hang on for that long? He wasn't sure. He was about to say "no thanks" when the image of Alisa popped into his head. The thought that she might give him an honest smile, more than her overly practiced, the-customer-is-right smile, gave him a jolt. He had no business thinking about that. Or wanting it.

"The job comes with a rent-free room at the motel next door. We own it like we own the diner," Mama added. "You get Sunday and Monday off, unless there's a crisis. And all you can eat here at the diner plus an hourly wage." She named a figure that made sense to Nick.

A tempting offer. "I've got my dog."

"I can't let him in the diner, and I wouldn't want him running loose around the grounds. But you can have him in the room with you as long as he behaves himself. On a leash otherwise."

Considering the job, he scratched his beard. He was definitely tired of being on the road. A clean room with a shower and free meals had a certain appeal.

Foolishly, he knew the real appeal was Alisa. He doubted she'd feel the same about him. Not if she knew the truth about how he'd spent the past three years in prison for a barroom brawl. One of the many fights he'd gotten into, part of his battle with PTSD.

"I sometimes get restless and need to move on. I wouldn't want to leave you in the lurch."

Shrugging, Mama grabbed the porch railing and pulled herself up. "If you don't steal me blind in the meantime, and I don't think you will or I wouldn't have offered you the job, I won't be any worse off than I am now with Jake gone."

That was true. He didn't have to feel pressured to stay.

Slowly, he stood. "Okay, I'll take your job."

She smiled, and he had the feeling she wanted to

pat his cheek again or hug him. It had been a long time since anyone had wanted to do that, which made him feel strange and oddly vulnerable.

"I've got a retired couple managing the motel. Frank and Helen Scotto. You'll be doing some work for them—changing lightbulbs, maybe a few repairs, nothing heavy. And if I have anything break down here at the diner, I'll let you know."

"Sounds good."

"Tell Frank or Helen to fix you up with a room. You can start work in the morning after breakfast."

He scratched his beard again. "Could I start a little late tomorrow? I'd like to get some of this fur off me."

"Good idea. Guess we'd all like to see what you look like under that mop you're wearing." Her eyes, the same deep blue shade as Alisa's, twinkled, and she laughed. "Ned Turner's the barber. He's a block up the road on the left hand side. He's got one of those red-and-white poles out front. Opens at eight."

"I'll find him."

She stooped to pick up his plate and the dog's. "I'll see you in the morning."

"Thank you, Mrs. Machak. I appreciate the job. And supper."

Her brows rose. "Mama, remember?"

He chuckled low in his chest. "Yes, Mama."

As Mama vanished into the kitchen, his laughter evaporated and a knot of fear twisted in his stomach. He knew he didn't dare get too comfortable here in Bear Lake. He'd be moving on soon, a residual problem left over from his abbreviated tour in Afghanistan along with the irrational fear that drove him.

## *Chapter Three*

Nick pulled open the drapes on the sliding glass door in the motel room. On the second floor at the back of the building, it had a small balcony and an angled look at the diner and a clear view to the west. A perfect place to watch the sun go down, and with the drapes open he wouldn't feel like the walls were closing in on him.

He turned back to scan the room. A queen-size bed covered with a forest-green quilt. Two pine-wood end tables and a matching low chest of drawers. A small flat-screen TV. Pretty standard motel fare but he'd stayed in worse. Like an eight-foot by eight-foot prison cell.

"What do you think, Rags? Home sweet home?" For a few days. Maybe a couple of weeks. It couldn't hurt to stay put for a while.

Without responding, Rags did his sniffing thing. In every new spot they'd stopped, the dog had to investigate the area thoroughly. Nick had no idea what Rags expected to find, but he sure was looking hard for it. Maybe he was searching for the trail of the family who had left him stranded in Colorado.

Nick knew where his own family was, what was left of it anyway. He had no plans to track his father down again.

He should have known better than to try.

His old man had never had time for him. And Nick had learned to keep his distance when his dad was drinking. At least until he was old enough and big enough to hold his own. After that, his old man had left him alone.

Opening the sliding glass door, he stepped out onto the balcony. Rags followed him and sat down, peering across the parking lot at the diner. The faintest hint of hamburgers on the grill drifted on a light breeze.

Nick wondered which of the upstairs rooms belonged to Alisa. She sure hadn't wandered far from home. And where was her son's father? He hadn't seen any sign of a husband around the place. Maybe he worked somewhere else.

Or maybe he'd moved on. She wasn't wearing a ring.

*None of your business, Carbini.*

"Come on, Rags. Let's get our gear from the truck and then we'll go looking for some regular dog food for you and a regular leash instead of that ol' rope I've been using."

Rags whined.

"Yeah, I know. You'd rather run around on your own." He shooed the dog back inside and closed the door. "But Mama says that's a no go. She doesn't want you running off her customers." He didn't think Alisa wanted Rags playing with her son either. He'd guess Greg would think otherwise.

The Thursday night crowd at the diner had thinned by eight-thirty.

"Good night, Alisa." Larry Cornwall, the high school football coach, tipped his cap as he was about to leave. "I'm still waiting for you to say yes to going to the Harvest Festival with me."

She shot him a grin. "Larry, you know how busy I am on Saturday nights." He'd been asking her out ever since he moved to town three years ago. For reasons that annoyed Mama, Alisa had always refused his invitations.

"The festival's a good cause. Football team needs your support."

"I'll make sure to get a check in the mail to you soon."

Frowning, he shook his head. "One of these days I'll wear you down, and you'll say yes just to get rid of me."

She laughed. "Have a good evening, Larry."

Alisa waved goodbye to him. She turned to straighten the menus and slipped them into place beside the cash register.

"I'm going to call it a night," she said to Jolene, who was working the evening shift. An attractive woman in her thirties with two children and a husband who worked for the state highway system, Jolene was unfailingly chipper. In addition to her, Tricia, a sweet teenager who worked part-time, was waiting tables. The two of them could handle the thinning crowd.

"Time to put Greg to bed, huh?" Jolene asked.

"Working the number of hours I do, bedtime is about the only chance I get to spend with him." A reality that gave her a large dose of guilt, yet she couldn't seem to figure out how to change the situation. She couldn't leave Mama to run the whole diner. There had been signs lately that her mother's arthritis was beginning to bother her.

"Whatever you're doing, he's a great little kid. Smart as a whip, too." She dumped out the coffee from the old pot and started to make a new one.

"I chalk that up to being very lucky, not to my parenting skills." Being a single parent had many disadvantages including the lack of enough time to give her child the attention he deserved. Of course, all of the staff and most of the regulars doted on him. But she wasn't sure that made up for her inattention. "I'll see you tomorrow. Say hello to Fred for me."

"Will do." Jolene shot her a bright smile. "And if you're asking, I think Larry would be a good catch for some woman. He's good-looking. Has a decent job."

"Guess I'm just not that woman." As nice as Larry was, she hadn't felt any spark with him. Without a spark, there couldn't be love. She wasn't going to settle for less than the real deal. If that meant she'd never have the kind of relationship her mother had had with Papa, so be it.

As Alisa took the stairs to the second floor, she removed the band that held her ponytail and shook her hair loose. Her aching feet loudly announced it had been another long day. Maybe she ought to promote Jolene to shift manager and hire an additional waitress. Then she could take on some of Mama's load in the kitchen.

The fly in the ointment would be the increased employee salaries they would have to pay. The profit margin for a restaurant was slim under the best of circumstances. These days the increasing price of food from the wholesaler kept the diner on a financial razor's edge.

The second-floor living quarters had three bedrooms, a cozy sitting room with a television rarely watched by anyone except Greg, a small kitchen and eating area. Considering they had a huge kitchen downstairs and ate most of their meals there, the upstairs kitchen didn't get used much. Greg's cereal for breakfast or a popcorn treat at night were about the limit of its use.

In the early days, before they'd bought the motel next door, Mama had rented out the rooms on the third floor. Now it was mostly unused except for storage.

She found Greg sprawled on the floor watching the Disney Channel. The arrival of satellite TV had been both a blessing and bane. She tried hard to limit Greg's TV time and the programs he saw. She wasn't always successful.

"Hey, buddy, how's it going?"

Without looking away from the TV screen, he said, "Fine."

Little boys were often inarticulate and very adept at ignoring their mothers. "So I'm planning a trip to Africa. I'm leaving in the morning. Want to come along?"

A pair of matching frown lines formed above his eyebrows. Belatedly he glanced up at Alisa. "Uh? Where are you going?"

She chuckled, sat down beside him on the floor and ruffled his curly hair. "Nowhere. But you're going to go get your pajamas on and get ready for bed."

"Ah, Mom. Can't I watch the end of this? It's almost over."

"How about you get your pajamas and change in here? When the show's over you can brush your teeth."

"Can I wait until the next commercial?"

Alisa rolled her eyes. Her son was going to grow up to be a big-time negotiator, maybe even someone who negotiated treaties with foreign countries. He always wanted to get a little more of whatever was being discussed. He usually got his way, too.

Of course, that was her fault. She hated to deny him anything.

She wondered if it would be different if he had a father who set the rules. Not that Ben, the drifter who had deserted her, would have provided much of a role model or been a disciplinarian. She'd had word a few years ago that he'd been killed in a rodeo accident. Although she felt bad that he had died so young, he never would have been a factor in Greg's life anyway. His loss.

The commercial started. Good to his word, Greg hopped up and dashed into his room.

Alisa stood as well. She strolled over to the window to close the curtains. Lighted windows in the Pine Tree Inn across the parking lot indicated they had nearly full occupancy. Idly she wondered which room was Nick's. And how long he'd stick around.

Not long, she imagined, giving the curtains a hard tug.

No way was she going to build a fantasy of happily-ever-after with another drifter.

The curtains hung up on something. She was about to give them another jerk when she saw the figure of a man standing behind the motel.

Squinting, she realized two things. First, despite the shadows she recognized the man was Nick. Second, he had balanced a stick or bar between two trees and was doing chin-ups one after another. His dog sat nearby watching Nick's every move.

A moment later, he dropped to the ground and started doing push-ups. One, two, three…

No wonder Nick seemed so strong, his arms so muscular. He was seriously into physical fitness.

Shaking her head, she finished closing the curtains. What was it, she wondered, that drove a drifter to push himself so hard physically?

Nick finished his workout. Despite the cool air, he was sweating from every pour. His muscles screamed from the exertion. He barely had enough energy to get to his feet.

Physically exhausted, he'd take a shower and hit the sack. Maybe with a firm mattress beneath him and clean Montana air to breathe, he'd sleep through until morning. Assuming the titanium rod and screws in his left leg didn't put up a battle.

"Come on, Rags. Let's call it a night."

They climbed the stairs to the second floor. Nick let the dog into the room and threw the deadbolt on the door.

It didn't take him long to shower and get into bed. He smiled at the feel of the crisp sheets, the stack of pillows beneath his head and the silence outside the sliding glass door. *You're coming up in the world, Carbini.*

After making a few revolutions in order to pick exactly the right spot, Rags settled down on the floor next to the bed.

Not much time had passed when the dream started. Distant explosions. Small arms fire. Men shouting orders.

Running feet. Bullets coming closer. Fear burning in his gut. Screams of pain.

Nick turned restlessly on the bed. He couldn't run. He couldn't leave his men. They were injured. Dying. He had to help.

He bolted upright, fully awake, covered with sweat. Rags with his paws on the bed, whining pitifully.

He wrapped his arms around the dog. "Good dog," he whispered, his voice husky with residual fear. Rags had awakened him before the worst of the dream could overwhelm him. The memory of his cowardice.

Lying back down, he stared up at the ceiling as his breathing slowed. Idly, he tangled his fingers in Rags's fur. He'd be all right now. The worst was over. Until tomorrow night.

The following morning, Nick got up at dawn to run with his dog, the air clear, the temperature autumn-crisp. Invigorating.

He showered and walked into town. He found the barbershop easily. Waiting for the shop to open, he tied Rags's leash to a streetlamp. "Sorry, buddy. You have to stay outside."

At that moment, Ned Turner arrived to unlock the door. "You coming in for a haircut, sergeant?"

"That's the plan."

"Bring your dog inside. No need for him to stay out here all by himself." A tall, slender man with graying hair, Ned opened the door wide. "Welcome to Bear Lake."

"Thank you." It wasn't often Nick had been called sergeant in the past few years, although the insignia of his former rank was obvious on his jacket.

When Nick saw the military insignias plastered all over the barbershop walls and photos of army platoons, plus a shelf full of coffee mugs with unit insignias, including one mug with the chaplain's cross, he realized why. Ned was former military himself and easily recognized the staff sergeant stripes on his army jacket.

Nick looped Rags's leash over the arm of one of the chairs that lined the wall. "Stay."

Rags sat. His eyes remained alert, riveted on Nick.

"What was your unit?" Ned flipped on the lights.

Nick shrugged out of his jacket and hung it on a coatrack. "Fifth Infantry. Stationed at Kandahar." Until the army decided to send him to an outlying camp to feed the troops. When al Qaeda overran the camp, Nick got an unplanned flight out to the U.S. hospital in Germany. He was luckier than most of the guys he worked with who went home in a box. Including his best buddy, Hank.

He squeezed his eyes shut momentarily to banish the image of smeared blood across stainless steel kitchen appliances where so many had died.

Ned gestured toward the barber chair. "I'm First Infantry. Served in 'Nam from '68 to '70."

"That was a tough war."

"They all are." He placed a cape around Nick's shoulders and ran a comb through his hair. "So what'll it be? Trim?"

"The whole shebang, shave and a haircut. I'm helping Mama out at the diner for a week or so as handyman. Figure I ought to at least look respectable when I'm working around the place." He smiled slightly. Alisa might appreciate a cleaned-up handyman, too, though she was unlikely to admit it.

"If you're working for Mama Machak, you better toe the line," Ned commented. "She's a pretty special lady around Bear Lake. Her daughter, too."

"I'll try to remember that." Nick didn't doubt for a moment that the townspeople would take Mama's side if a stranger tried to cross her. Maybe that's what made Bear Lake a good place to live.

Except he wasn't looking for a place to settle down.

As Ned began working on him, a couple of fellows came into the shop. One began making a pot of coffee without asking. The other gave Rags a couple of pats then picked up the morning newspaper.

"Mitchell there behind the newspaper served in Iraq," Ned said, snipping at Nick's hair with his scissors. "The guy with the coffee habit is Ward. He's a marine, but we let him hang out with us army types anyway."

Ward shot a look over his shoulder. "Only 'cause you know I could take you out with my hands tied behind my back."

Mitchell and Ned laughed.

"We got ourselves our own veterans group." Ned brushed loose hair off Nick's shoulders. "Nothing formal, you understand. We meet every Wednesday night in my back room. Half a dozen or so, some who are still shaking off the memories of whatever war they were fighting. 'Nam, Iraq, Afghanistan, it's all the same for us grunts when we come home. If you're around next Wednesday, come on by."

Surprised by the invitation, Nick said, "I'll keep that in mind." He wasn't sure he'd be in Bear Lake that long, or whether he'd want to sit in with a bunch of vets who probably spent their time complaining about the government.

But the chaplain at the Louisiana State Prison where he'd spent three years for assault in a barroom brawl had put together a cadre of vets. They were like him—still having flashbacks. It had helped to know he wasn't the only one. But it hadn't changed anything.

Still, he hadn't figured out what God's plan was for him. Or if it had anything to do with coming back to Bear Lake.

A half hour later, Nick left the barbershop. His face felt naked, and he was ready for one of Mama's hearty breakfasts.

He hated to do it, but knew he had to tie Rags up this time. Mama's orders. So he secured the leash to a post at the side of the diner and told the dog to stay.

Alisa grabbed a menu as a stranger walked into the diner. She greeted him with her usual smile. "Good morning. Would you like a table? Or would you rather sit at the counter?" Men alone often wanted to eat at the counter so they could visit with the waitress as she passed by.

"The counter will do."

Alisa's mouth dropped open. She knew that voice but not the face. "Nick?" Her voice caught.

He flashed her a set of white teeth. "Early morning visit to the barber."

"Y…yes, I can see that." From the third grader she'd known, Nick Carbini had grown into a striking man with a strong jaw, full lips and a classic nose. His beard and shaggy hair had been hiding a man who could cause a woman's heart to flutter. Well, most women, she supposed. But not her. Absolutely not her.

All business, she gestured toward the counter. "Take your pick." Walking behind the counter, she placed a menu in front of him. "Coffee?"

"Please. Black."

She hesitated, staring at him longer than necessary, noting the teasing glint in his incredible eyes, before wheeling around to the get the coffeepot. Now that he'd shaved and had his jet-black hair cut in a way that emphasized the natural waves, he was more dangerous than ever.

What woman wouldn't be tempted to weave her fingers through his hair?

"Here you go." She poured a mug of coffee and set it in front of him.

"You work long hours," he commented. "Through

the dinner hour last night and now up for the breakfast shift."

"We get a pretty big rush until ten o'clock. Then I take a break until it's time to set up for dinner."

"Unless you have to chop wood."

"Well, yes. Things do come up." After years of serving customers, she suddenly didn't know what to do with the coffeepot she still held in her hand. She licked her lips. Set the pot down on the counter. "Do you know what you want for breakfast? Or do you need a minute?" She was the one who needed a minute to get her head on straight. Whatever was wrong with her?

"How 'bout a couple of over easy eggs, hash browns and wheat toast?"

"Coming right up." She returned the coffeepot to the warmer and started to write up Nick's order. Her pencil poised over the order pad, she stopped. Her mind had gone blank. Totally empty of everything except his eyes and how he'd looked at her. For the life of her, she couldn't remember what he'd ordered.

She gnawed on her lower lip. There was no reason for her to go brain-dead simply because the man had gotten a shave and a haircut.

Her face flamed as she turned to ask him to repeat his order, and that's when her brain finally shifted back into gear. *Over easy eggs, hash browns and wheat toast.* She quickly wrote down the order and passed it through to Billy Newton, the morning short-order cook.

Plucking up the coffeepot, she skirted the counter—and Nick—refilling customers' cups and chatting with the regulars.

A large booth near the kitchen door was permanently reserved for the "old duffers" group, men whom she'd known all of her life and were now retired. They came in to visit and gossip, drinking gallons of coffee and putting together thousand-piece jigsaw puzzles that remained spread out on the table until they were completed.

"Good morning, gentlemen." She held up the coffeepot, and two of the four men seated at the table slid their mugs toward her for refills. "How's the world today?"

"State's talking about widening the back road to Plains to make an alternate route for tourists." Ezra Cummings was the senior member of the group, still agile and mentally quick at the age of ninety-two.

"Ain't worth it," Abe, a retired lumberman, complained. "Ought to save the tax money and send them tourists back where they come from."

"Don't send them all back, Abe." Alisa set the pot down, picked up a piece of the puzzle, studied it a moment then fit it in right where it belonged in the waterfall part of the woodland scene. "Remember Mama and I need those tourist dollars to keep afloat." She spied another puzzle piece and dropped it into place.

The old duffers nodded their approval. Alisa had been doing jigsaw puzzles for as long as she could remember. By now, finding the right spot for the oddly curved and angled puzzle tiles was instinctive.

She carried the pot over to Dr. McCandless, who had been her pediatrician when she was young and now was Greg's. He was sitting alone in a booth. Sometimes Mama came out to join him for breakfast.

"Good morning, doctor. Can I fill it up for you?"

"Just halfway. My doctor says I should ease up on the caffeine."

"We do have decaf, if you'd rather."

"Can't see the sense of drinking coffee if it doesn't have a little kick to it." His youthful smile crinkled the corners of his pale blue eyes and made them twinkle. A longtime widower, it was amazing some woman hadn't latched on to him by now.

By the time she returned the coffeepot to the warmer, Billy had Nick's order ready. She considered asking Dotty, who was serving the table section, to deliver Nick's breakfast to him at the counter. But her pride, a stubborn streak much like her mother's, wouldn't let her succumb to acting like a coward.

"Two eggs over easy, hash browns and toast."

She slid the plate in front of him. "Ketchup's right here on the counter. Jam too." She slid the jam closer to him. "Anything else you need?"

"It looks good. I could use a coffee refill if you have time."

"No problem." Of course she had the time. He could see no one else was sitting at the counter. So why did he have to be so nice and polite? He'd been polite as a kid, too. Never teasing the girls or chasing them like some of the boys did. One time he'd even picked up a book that she had knocked off her desk onto the floor. After that the girls had all started dropping their books or pencils or some silly thing to get his attention.

He'd been unfailingly kind even though he'd known what they were up to.

Shaking her head, she tried to wipe away the memory. Just because he'd been a polite kid didn't mean anything to her now. People changed a lot in twenty years.

Mama came out from the kitchen wearing a butcher apron and her graying hair in a net. "Alisa, have you seen Nick?" She spied him at the counter. "Well, now, aren't you the handsome thing without all those whiskers."

His cheeks deepened to a rich shade of red. He dipped his head, focusing on scooping up a bit of egg yolk with his toast.

"No rush, young man," Mama said. "Finish your

breakfast. Then I'd like you to try to fix those loose boards on the back steps. I noticed last night that they were wobbly. Don't want anybody to fall, particularly when they get iced up this winter."

"I'd be happy to give it a try."

"Alisa, honey, you can show Nick where we keep the tools when he's ready."

Her stomach sank. Perfect. Just what she wanted to do. Spend more time in Nick's company. Not.

# *Chapter Four*

Excruciatingly aware of Nick and his dog following her, Alisa led them to the equipment shed behind the diner. She heard his footsteps on the gravel. Caught the faint scent of his tangy aftershave on the breeze. Felt his eyes boring a hole into her back.

Straightening her spine, she gave her hair a little toss as she keyed the padlock open and slid the door aside. There was nothing to be nervous about. She'd been in this shed for one reason or another with Jake Domino any number of times.

Nick Carbini wasn't any different. They were both handymen. Or so she told herself as Nick brushed past her into the shed, planting himself in the dim light at the center of the garage-size structure.

Rags stretched out his leash to investigate on his own.

"You've got lots of equipment," he commented, checking out their four-wheel drive Jeep and the old aluminum fishing boat on a trailer beside it. Her father had named it *Dreamer* because of his dream to own his own business.

She turned on the overhead lights. "We use the Jeep to clear our own parking lot when it snows and to get around town when we need to in winter. In the summer, we can drag a tiller for the small garden where we raise fresh vegetables."

"Ah, that's why the julienne squash tasted so good last night. Nothing beats from-garden-to-table fresh vegetables."

"We're pretty much at the tail end of the vegetable garden now." It surprised her that he'd noticed the fresh produce. Most men wolfed down their meal without even tasting it. Apparently Nick took a little more time with his dinner.

"The hand tools are to your left." Hammers, hand saws, screwdrivers, and pliers hung neatly on a Peg-Board. "Have you done much carpentry work?"

"One summer when I was a teenager I got o construction crew as a helper."

"Is that what you do for a living? Construction?" She could have bitten her tongue for asking, but the words had simply popped out of her mouth. Her curiosity had gotten the best of her.

He poked around checking out the power tools

next to the workbench and hefted a power saw. "Not usually. I only lasted on the job for a couple of weeks. I dropped a load of two-by-fours on the boss's foot. He wasn't real happy with me."

"Guess that was long after you moved away from Bear Lake."

He turned slowly to look at her. "You know I used to live here?"

Trying for casual, she leaned back against the Jeep and crossed her arms. "We were in the same third-grade class."

He returned the power saw to its place and crossed the shed to her. He studied her face, but there was no recognition in his eyes.

An irritating sense of disappointment tightened her lips.

"That was a long time ago," he said.

"Mama remembered your family."

He snorted a disparaging sound. "And she still hired me?"

"She remembers you being a nice kid." So did Alisa, although she wasn't about to admit that.

He looked at her again and shook his head. "I'm sure if I'd stuck around here a few years longer, I would have remembered you. You're not a woman a man would easily forget."

But boys rarely remembered skinny girls with stringy hair and massive gaps between their front teeth, which Alisa eventually eliminated with braces.

She stepped aside, trying to put more space between them. Far enough so that she couldn't feel his eyes skimming over her face making her cheeks flush and her breath catch. "Well, help yourself to whatever tools you need to fix the steps. Just be sure to lock up the shed when you're done."

"You got it."

Exiting as quickly as she could, she hurried back to the diner. *Not a woman a man would easily forget.* Did he mean that? Or was he simply being polite? A throwaway compliment?

What difference would it make either way? She liked her life the way it was. Things were comfortable. Predictable. Perfect for her.

During the prelunch lull, she found her mother at her desk in the kitchen working out her order for the next day from the restaurant supply delivery service.

"I wish you hadn't hired that man," she said.

Mama glanced up at her. "What man?"

"You know what man I mean. Our new handyman."

"Ah, you mean Nick. Why should I not have hired him?"

"Well, because..." Unable to think of a logical reason, she plopped down in the chair beside the desk.

"Because he makes you nervous?" Mama provided.

"Of course not. It's just that… Well, he doesn't really have any construction experience. He won't have any idea how to fix the steps."

"He's a smart man. He'll figure it out."

Leaning back in the chair, Alisa sighed.

"What is it, my little princess?" Mama asked softly, using the words Alisa's father had called her. "Is it that you are attracted to Nick?"

"Certainly not." She folded her arms across her chest. "He only showed up yesterday. He'll be gone soon. Why would I be attracted to a man like that?" *Another drifter.*

Looking at Alisa with a mother's probing eye, Mama said, "I think you are afraid to feel something for a man."

"That's nonsense."

"Ever since Ben, you will have nothing to do with any man. You ignore them. Or you put on a phony smile and laugh off their advances. You're thirty years old. At your age, you should be thinking about—"

"Mama, I'm perfectly happy just as I am. I don't need a man. I've got Greg and I've got you. That's all the family I need." Her voice shaking, she stood. "As for the men around here, they're either married, divorced or can't manage an intelligent conversation for more than two seconds."

"Larry Cornwall is a smart man. He has a college degree."

"He's a jock, Mama. He talks about fullbacks and tailbacks and running the end around something. He spends his spare time watching reruns of college games. That hardly makes for an intellectual conversation."

"So you say. But it may be that Nick Carbini is different than other men you have met. Maybe there's a reason God brought him back home."

"Don't count on it. Besides, drifters don't have a home." Without saying another word, Alisa marched out of the kitchen. What a ridiculous thing for her mother to say. That she was *afraid* of men? Not for a moment. She could do anything a man could do. Chop wood. Plow snow from their parking lot. She could probably fix the porch steps if she were so inclined.

It was just that Nick made her…nervous.

She'd strayed from God's path once, which left her with a heartache and a child born out of wedlock. Although she would never regret having Greg, she had no intention of making that mistake again.

Which was precisely why Nick made her so nervous. If she weakened even a little, she might not be able to stop from making another serious error in judgment. A woman didn't fall into a man's arms simply because she was attracted to his dark good looks and the hint of loneliness in his eyes. That would only lead to heartache.

Wood rot was the problem on the bottom two steps. Not simply the bolts that held the step in place loosening.

Nick had found some wood that matched the existing steps and cut it to length. There had even been a jar full of the bolts in the shed that he needed. Now he was drilling holes for the new bolts.

"Hey, mister."

Silencing the drill, Nick looked up. "Hey, Greg. You can call me Nick, if you want."

"'Kay."

"How was school?"

"Same ol'. What're you doing?"

Nick sat back on his haunches. "Fixing these steps. They were wobbly."

The boy eyed the new wood. "Can I help?"

Nick gave some thought to whether Alisa would approve or not. "Maybe when I put the sealer on the new wood you could help." A boy needed to feel useful, not ignored.

The youngster shifted from one foot to the other, then eased over to Rags, who was tied up a few feet away. "Maybe I could play with Rags while I'm waiting."

Nick's lips twitched into a smile. "I think Rags would like that a lot."

"Great." He tossed his backpack aside and dropped to his knees, roughing up Rags's coat and scratching him behind his ears. Eager to return the greeting, Rags licked Greg's face, which resulted in high-pitched giggles. Unhooking the leash, Greg said, "Come on, boy. Let's find a stick."

Smiling, Nick watched the two of them race off, Rags in the lead, happy at last to be able to run free.

He'd never had a dog as a kid. The closest he'd come to having a pet was a goldfish he'd won at a school carnival. The poor fish—he'd named him Oscar—hadn't lasted long. One morning Nick had found him on the floor. Oscar had apparently jumped out of his bowl during the night. Nick had wanted to bury him in the backyard, but his dad made him flush the fish down the toilet.

It didn't matter. Either way, Oscar was dead. Nick wasn't allowed to cry.

He wrestled the new steps into place and tightened down the bolts. The newly cut wood smelled clean and fresh. He could understand why a man would want to work with his hands building things. Things that lasted.

Alisa stepped out onto the porch and hesitated

a moment checking out Nick's work. Then she let her gaze travel to Greg and Rags who were romping through the high grass.

"Greg! Time to come in."

The boy circled around before racing Rags back to the diner. He slid to a stop, breathing hard. Rags dropped to the ground panting. Both boy and dog had worn themselves out. At least momentarily.

"I was worried about you," Alisa said. "You were late getting home."

"I was playing with Rags."

"So I gather. Come on in. You can have a snack before you do your homework."

"It's Friday, Mom. I don't have any homework."

"Well, come in anyway, honey. I'll find you—"

"I can't, Mom. Nick said I could help him put sealer on the step."

Her gaze dropped pointedly to Nick, who was squatting on the bottom step. "He did?"

He lifted his shoulders in a casual shrug. "The bare wood has to be sealed or it will absorb rain and snow. You'd have to replace the steps all over again in a couple of years."

"I know that."

Nick grinned. "Of course you do."

She glowered at him. Nick figured she didn't like to be teased, but it was kind of fun anyway, seeing her get all flustered. Her cheeks turned pink with a blush.

"If he's going to help," Nick said, "might be good if he changed into old jeans and a shirt. Sealer can get pretty messy."

Greg snatched up his backpack. "Can I, Mom? Can I?"

She sighed in defeat. "I suppose."

"Thanks, Mom." The boy leaped up the steps and burst in through the door.

Resting her hand on the railing, she shook her head and frowned. "It's all right if he helps you some, but I don't want my son to get…attached to you."

A sharp pain of regret stabbed Nick in the chest. "You don't have to worry. I won't be around that long."

Her gaze skittered away from Nick. "I know. That's exactly why I don't want him to get too friendly with you."

"Guess your husband would object, too."

Her gaze snapped back to him. She bristled. "I don't have a husband."

"I wondered about that." It didn't seem right that such a good-looking woman didn't have a husband. A father for her son. "Guess the guys around here are all blind and half-stupid for not latching on to a good thing when it's right in front of their noses."

She brought herself up to all of her five-feet-five height and lifted her chin. "Mr. Carbini, I'll have you know I am not the kind of woman who *latches* on to any man who just happens to be handy. Nor do they *latch* onto me. Now, if you'll excuse me, I'm going to see that Greg changes into something appropriate for painting the porch steps." Doing an abrupt about-face, she marched into the diner.

Thoughtfully, Nick tilted his head. She was one proud lady. Chances were good all that pride was hiding one giant hurt that hadn't ever healed.

If Nick knew for sure who had done the hurting, he'd be happy to take the fellow into the woodshed and do a little attitude correcting on Alisa's behalf.

Except chances were also good that she wouldn't appreciate him being the one standing up for her. Not if she knew about his past.

Nick got back to work, and it wasn't long before Greg reappeared at the back porch.

"I'm ready!" He wore jeans with a tear in them, a faded blue T-shirt and an eager smile.

"Okay, Greg. Let's see if your mom has a can of sealer and some paintbrushes in the equipment shed."

Nick hadn't put Rags back on his leash after Greg went inside to change. Now the dog trotted beside the boy, probably in the hope a suitable fetch stick would appear.

"You know where your mom keeps the paints?"

"In the back." The boy dashed ahead, Rags on his heels.

Nick sauntered after them. Gallon paint containers lined four shelves across half the back wall. Scanning the labels, Nick found what he was looking for, a half-full can of sealer. He pried open the lid.

"Looks good. Now, how 'bout brushes?"

Greg picked out a couple of nice, wide brushes, and they carried the paint and brushes back to the steps.

While Nick was stirring the sealer, Greg said, "Want to hear a joke?"

Nick lifted his brows. "You sure it's a good one?"

"Yeah, everybody laughs. Why did the elephant paint her toenails red?"

Suppressing a groan, Nick said, "I don't know, kid. Why did the elephant paint her toenails red?"

"Because she wanted to hide in a field of strawberries."

Nick's groan escaped, followed by a chuckle. "That's pretty good. Now, how 'bout we get to work."

Starting Greg at one end of the upper step, Nick showed the boy how to brush on the sealer without letting it drip. He started on the other end working toward the middle.

As he worked, he remembered as a kid he used to tell silly jokes. He was pretty shy, and telling a joke helped him not to feel like a dork.

"Okay, I've got a joke for you," Nick said, pulling up an old groaner from deep in his memory. "Knock knock."

Greg grinned. "Who's there?"

"Woo."

"Woo who?"

"Now don't get so excited. It's just a knock knock joke."

Greg laughed out loud. "That's a good one, Nick. I'm going to tell that one to Mom."

"You do that, son." Nick smoothed the sealer across the step. He'd like to see Alisa laugh. Her smile would light up the whole Bear Lake valley like the sun rising over the mountains.

Idly he wondered when he had stopped telling jokes and became a loner instead. Maybe when he and his dad moved away from Bear Lake.

On Friday nights, Alisa let Greg stay up later than on school nights. After he put on his pajamas, he came and plopped down on the couch next to her where she'd been trying to read a book.

"You wanna hear a joke, Mom? Nick told me a new one."

She tensed and closed her book. "Nick told you a joke?"

"Yeah. While we were painting the steps. I think he likes me."

Swallowing hard, she finger-brushed his hair,

trying to tame the cowlicks. "Of course he likes you. Everybody likes you."

Squirming away, he looked at her with troubled eyes. "If everybody likes me, how come my dad didn't stick around? How come he left before I was even born?" His chin trembled ever so slightly.

"Sweetie, your father—" A man she'd come to think of as no more than a sperm donor. "—He didn't leave because of you. He left because he didn't want to take responsibility for anyone except himself. He was too selfish to be a good daddy. Because of that, he's the one who missed out on seeing you grow into such a smart kid. A handsome one, too."

Greg wrinkled his nose. "Nick is a responsible man, isn't he? I mean, he's fixing the steps for Mama and all."

Mentally, she grimaced. Her son was already falling under Nick's spell. "Greg, honey, Nick is just filling in for Jake. He'll be gone soon. You know that."

"Well, he might stay." His lower lip pushed out. "If he liked it here a lot, he'd stay, wouldn't he?"

Tears burned at the back of her eyes, and she hugged her son. "If he leaves, it won't be because of you. I promise." *It will be because a drifter can't stay in one place too long. It's part of their nature.*

Greg pulled away from her. "So do you want to hear the joke he told me?"

"Sure. Let me have it, munchkin."

To her dismay, it was one of Nick's old knock knock jokes from their grade-school days. She laughed but her heart wasn't in it. Hadn't the man learned anything new in the last twenty years?

And why did it hurt so much to know he and his silly jokes would be moving on soon?

Alisa had put Greg to bed nearly an hour ago. There was nothing on TV she wanted to watch. The book she'd been reading wasn't holding her interest, and the jigsaw puzzle spread out on the kitchen table wasn't calling her.

Mama had already retired for the night. The hum of customers downstairs had quieted to a low murmur. She could go down, see if any locals were around, join them for a cup of coffee and some conversation.

Unfortunately, she was too restless to even consider that option and it bugged her.

*It was all Nick's fault!* Why on earth had he told Greg that silly knock knock joke? All it did was make her remember him as a boy eager to get the approval of his classmates. He'd already had her approval, which he hadn't even noticed.

In spite of her best intentions, she pulled the living room curtain aside to peek outside.

He was there again, standing out beyond the end

of the motel, his back to the diner, doing chin-ups on the bar stuck between two trees.

"This is ridiculous." Grabbing a jacket from the closet, she headed downstairs. She'd find out why he was so into muscle building.

Then she'd be able to sleep without thoughts of Nick Carbini running around in her head.

# *Chapter Five*

Alisa walked across the parking lot, approaching Nick quietly. She couldn't imagine how many chin-ups he'd already done. Still he moved steadily, like a valve in a well tuned engine. With each lift, his biceps flexed. Sweat dampened the back of his shirt.

The soft sounds he made when he pulled himself up again and again spoke of a determination to never quit.

As she drew closer, the dog spotted her and alerted.

Slowly, Nick turned his head toward her. Shadowed by the trees, she couldn't read his expression as he dropped to the ground.

"I'm sorry. I didn't mean to interrupt your routine." Of course, if she'd been thinking at all, she would have known he'd stop when she invaded his privacy.

"It's okay." He bent at the waist to catch his breath.

Rags trotted over to greet her. She scratched the top of his head, which got his tail wagging even faster than usual.

"You work out so hard," she said. "Are you planning to try out for Mr. America?"

He coughed what was meant to be a laugh. "Hardly. I try to wear myself out at night so I can sleep better."

She tugged the sides of her jacket together, although she wasn't that cold. "Does it work? There are nights when I could use a little help with that." Particularly since Nick arrived in town.

Her comment was greeted with such a long silence, she was about to tell him good-night and get back to where she belonged.

"Learning to do chin-ups and push-ups isn't so hard. You start easy. Do what you can, and each time you make yourself do a little more." He paused for a moment. "I could help you if you want." His voice was a mere whisper, no louder than the faint breeze in the treetops, and surprisingly intimate.

Heat prickled her skin. Her heart lurched and skipped a beat. A knot of panic formed in her stomach. She feared that Nick could teach her any number of things she'd be better off not knowing.

"That's okay. You'd probably rather do your own thing. Besides, I should go in. Check on Greg."

She took a backward step.

"Another time, then." In slow, careful steps, he closed the distance between them. "Whenever you're ready to give it a try."

"I, um, I don't mean to get personal, but I've noticed…is there a problem with your leg? It seems like—"

"My leg's fine now. Just a little limp sometimes if I'm especially tired and don't concentrate when I walk. I've got a titanium rod in there along with some screws. Plays havoc with the security folks at an airport."

She gasped. "How did you—"

"I took a few chunks of shrapnel in my leg in Afghanistan. It's better than what happened to some of my buddies."

Sympathy welled in her chest. "I'm so sorry, Nick. I had no idea." Aghast at the thought he'd been wounded in the war, she shook her head. "I really shouldn't have asked."

"It's no big deal."

"Of course it's a big deal. You're a war hero."

"No, Alisa. I'm nobody's idea of a hero." A hint of regret slipped into his voice.

She imagined Greg already thought of Nick as a hero without even knowing about his leg. How sad Nick couldn't think of himself that way.

He called his dog to his side. "Time for me to turn in. Some customer tried to run his fist through the wall in room 210." He gestured toward the motel. "Frank wants me to plaster the hole and paint the wall tomorrow."

"That'll keep you busy."

"That's why I'm here." He hesitated for one brief second. "Good night, Alisa. See you at breakfast."

He turned away from her. Walking without the slightest limp, he reached the motel stairs and climbed to the second floor.

Foolishly, she waited until the light went on in the last room on the floor. Now when she looked out her living room window, she'd know which room was Nick's. One small bit of information she'd be better off not knowing.

The next morning, as soon as Greg finished his breakfast of cereal and juice in the family kitchen, he was all set to find Nick.

"I'm sure he's busy working today," Alisa said. Her son's case of hero worship had certainly flourished in a matter of hours, like a potent virus. "He probably doesn't want you bothering him all the time."

"He liked it when I helped him yesterday."

True, Nick hadn't objected to Greg hanging around him. But that didn't mean he wanted Greg to become his constant companion. "Instead of helping Nick, why don't you call one of your friends? Maybe they could come over and play one of your video games and have lunch in the diner."

"Nah. That sounds boring." He stuffed his hands in the pockets of his jeans.

A week ago, playing his new video game had been at the top of Greg's to-do list. Now Nick had soared ahead on his priority list.

"I know what I can do!" Greg announced. A big grin creased his cheek. "If Nick's busy, I bet he'd like me to take Rags for a walk. Don't you think so, Mom? He'd want Rags to get some exercise, don't you think?"

Mentally rolling her eyes, Alisa caressed the back of her son's blond head. "Yes, I think he might like that. But if he says no, don't you dare beg or pester him. You understand?"

"Yeah, sure, Mom. I know that. You don't want me to bug him too much when he's working."

"That's right." She told him where he'd find Nick at the motel.

"'Kay. I'll see you later." With that, Greg dashed for the stairs, thundered down the steps. Alisa heard the back kitchen door slam behind him.

It wasn't long before she glanced outside and saw Greg and Rags on a leash running along the path that led behind the diner to the school a couple of blocks away. Greg whooped with excitement. Rags responded with eager barks, his tail waving in the air.

She sent up a quick prayer that her son wouldn't feel too brokenhearted when Nick and his dog drifted on to somewhere else.

Bucking herself up and intentionally putting a spring in her step, she went downstairs to help with the breakfast crowd. September weekends were prime time for fishermen to try their luck on Bear Lake. They liked to start the day with a hearty meal.

Saturday evening, Nick picked a church out of the yellow pages to attend Sunday morning. His family had never been churchgoers, but he'd come to realize over the past few years that he needed a higher power in his life. He still had a lot to learn about faith and the Lord's message.

While he was in Bear Lake, the Community Church sounded like a good place to seek answers and find inner peace.

The church was located a little west of town. The whitewashed building sat on about an acre of land. Nick pulled his truck into a spot in the gravel parking lot, which was filled with other pickups and SUVs, the preferred means of mountain transportation.

"Sorry, Rags." He let the dog out of the truck and hooked up his leash. He hadn't wanted to leave Rags on his own in the motel room or at the diner. "No dogs allowed in church. I'll have to tie you up to the bumper. Don't you worry, though. I'll be back as soon as I can. Let's hope the preacher isn't too long-winded." He set out a bowl of water and put an old throw rug down for Rags to lay on in the shade of the truck.

Just as he straightened upright, he heard Greg's voice.

"Hey, Mom, look! Nick's here and he's got Rags." Wearing new jeans and a fresh shirt, the boy came running toward him. "Hey, Nick. You're going to church this morning?"

Nick's lips hitched into a smile. "That's the plan."

"Great. You can sit with Mom. I gotta go to Sunday school." He dropped to his knees to pet Rags.

Nick met Alisa's gaze as she approached, then let his slide over her, from her blonde hair hanging loose around her shoulders to her toes, the nails painted bright pink peeking out from a pair of leather sandals. Instead of her usual slacks and simple blouse she wore at the diner, she had on a summery dress with a full skirt and short navy blue jacket. Very feminine. And appealing.

"Good morning," she said, her voice a little husky.

"Morning to you." The blue of her jacket accented the deep blue of her eyes. "Glad Mama lets you have some time off."

"Going to church every Sunday has always been

a part of my life. Mama's, too, but she was feeling extra tired this morning."

"Sorry to hear Mama's not feeling so good."

"She'll probably be better later."

"I'm kind of new to the church routine," he admitted.

Her brows rose slightly, but he didn't offer any explanation. He doubted she'd be impressed to learn where he had found the Lord—behind bars in a prison chapel that doubled as a recreation room for convicts and featured an all male choir.

The bell in the church steeple began to ring.

"Time to go in." Turning to Rags, he said, "Sit. Stay. I'll be back soon."

Greg hopped to his feet. "See you later, Rags. I gotta go see the guys." He dashed off without a goodbye to his mother or Nick.

Twisting her lips into an amused smile, Alisa said, "At Greg's age, his peers are more important than his aged mother."

Laughing, Nick instinctively cupped Alisa's elbow and they began walking toward the church entrance. He caught the scent of her perfume, something flowery and sweet. "You've got a long way to go before anyone would think of you as aged."

"I certainly hope so."

As they approached the large double doors, Nick reluctantly released his grip on Alisa's arm, her skin so soft and smooth she felt like velvet. After serving in the army and then landing in prison, he'd missed the softness of a woman. Her special scent.

A man in slacks and an open-collar shirt stepped forward and extended his hand "It's Nick, isn't it? We met at the barbershop."

Caught off guard for a moment, Nick searched for the guy's name as they shook hands. "Right. You're Ward. Used to be a marine."

"Once a marine, always a marine. Welcome to Bear Lake Community Church." He shifted his attention to Alisa. "Wife and kids and I plan to be at the diner after church. Potato pancakes all around."

She smiled and shook his hand. "I'll make sure we don't run out before you get there."

"Better not. You'd have a small riot on your hands."

Ward handed her the morning's program and offered one to Nick. "Hope to see you Wednesday night at Ned's."

"I'll see how it's going by then," he hedged, unwilling to make a commitment and not sure how long he'd be in town. Still, he'd lasted three days in Bear Lake. So far he hadn't had the urge to move on. That was a good sign.

No doubt Alisa had something to do with it. Which wasn't such a good sign.

* * *

Halfway down the aisle looking for a seat, Alisa glanced back over her shoulder, just checking to see if Nick was following her. Not that she thought he would. Or that he should. He'd probably pick a place to sit on his own.

She'd never expected to see him at church. Nor had she expected to see him looking so handsome in new jeans and a button-down white shirt with the collar open.

For a drifter, he looked way too appealing.

The fact that he knew Ward Cummings surprised her, too. How could Nick be making friends so fast? He'd only been in town three days.

Like with the workout business, maybe she'd been too quick to judge him.

She slipped into a pew, smiled at the couple seated nearby and sat down. She glanced around the chapel looking for friends. The sun sparkling through the stained-glass window behind the pulpit sprinkled colorful bits of confetti across the congregation.

Inhaling deeply, she bowed her head, making the effort to calm her mind and open herself to the Lord's presence. *Dear Lord, thank You for this beautiful day. Fill my heart and mind with peace. Watch over Mama and Greg. And Nick,* she added, surprising herself.

Without even looking up, she knew the moment

Nick entered her row of pews. She tensed. Goose flesh rose on her arms as he sat next to her. Not too close, but close enough that she was aware of the breadth of his shoulders, the firmness of his thighs stretching the dark blue denim of his jeans, the way he linked his strong fingers together between his knees and bowed his head.

*Oh, dear...* How was she supposed to concentrate on the church service with Nick sitting next to her? Or find the peace she usually did in church?

For years, she'd been praying that she would not succumb to temptation again. Then Nick drifted into town, which was bad enough. But here he was at church, tempting her to have wildly irrational thoughts about him staying in town and a future they might have together.

Utter nonsense. She knew better.

She gritted her teeth as the organ music crescendoed and the congregation rose for the first hymn.

Nick held out the hymnal, opened to the correct page, silently offering to share. She had no choice but to stand ever closer to him and grasp her side of the hymnal. Her shoulder brushed his, and she felt the heat of his body through his shirt and her cotton jacket. His baritone voice blended with her imperfect soprano, his words ringing with the power of welcoming God's bright morning sunlight.

When they finished the hymn, she made it a

point to reestablish a modicum of distance between them. Still, his warmth on her arm lingered.

Her nerves on edge, the service seemed to drag. In his sermon, Pastor Walker waxed on for what felt like an hour yet she could barely concentrate or absorb his message of God's love and forgiveness. She wanted to be somewhere else. Anywhere Nick Carbini wasn't.

She'd never been so relieved to hear the final prayer. She stood quickly. Nick moved more slowly.

"So are you going back to the diner?" he asked, waiting to cup her elbow again, easing her up the aisle toward the exit.

"I usually do." For a drifter, he certainly knew how to act like a gentleman.

"I thought I might drive around a little. See if I can find the old house where I lived as a kid. Kind of get reacquainted with the town."

"Well, have a pleasant afternoon."

Once outside, she scooted away from him, drew a deep breath of fresh air and looked around the milling crowd of church goers for Greg. He was nowhere in sight, which was odd. Other children from the Sunday School were rejoining their parents. But no Greg.

She frowned. Where could he have—

*The dog!* Of course he'd make a beeline for Rags the moment he got out of class.

She made her way through the crowd, her progress slow as friends greeted her. Finally she escaped and headed for Nick's truck. She wasn't happy that Greg had taken off without waiting for her. He knew better than that.

She spotted him with Nick. And the dog, of course. Her stomach churned. That man had gotten her stirred up enough for one day. She didn't need him and his dog taking over her son's life.

"Hey, Mom," Greg shouted, grinning at her. Rags's front paws rested on her son's shoulders, his tail wagging as he licked the boy's face. "Nick wants to explore Bear Lake. Can we show him around? Can we?"

*No!* "Gregory, when I came out of church I couldn't find you." She used the stern voice her son would recognize as trouble. "You should have waited for me instead of running off over here."

He lifted the dog's paws from his shoulders and put him down. "I thought you'd know where I'd gone."

"You think I'm a mind reader?"

His expression turned petulant. "Sometimes you are."

"Not nearly often enough, apparently."

Grabbing the dog's collar, Nick tugged Rags to his side. "I'm sorry. I should have realized you'd be looking for Greg and sent him back to find you."

"My son is not your responsibility. He's old enough to know better himself." She hooked her hand over his shoulder. "Come on, Greg. We'd better get back to the diner to help Mama. You know she wasn't feeling well this morning."

He shot her a pleading look. "You could go home, and I can show Nick around. I know where stuff is."

Nick interceded. "Maybe another time, Greg. It's better you do what your mother says."

Alisa had to give him credit for taking her side, not undermining her orders. Even so, she wished she weren't discovering how *nice* he was. At this rate, when Nick left town she'd miss him almost as much as Greg would.

Turning her back on Nick, she steeled her heart and vowed that wasn't going to happen. Not this time.

Nick stood by his truck until he saw Alisa drive off with her son. She was one strong lady. A woman who didn't have much use for him, which made her smart, too. But standing next to her in church, holding the hymnal together, catching the lemony scent of her hair, had reached something down deep in him. A longing. A need that he'd never before recognized.

A need he had to put back in its box and firmly close the lid.

Rags shifted, alerting to someone behind Nick. He turned around to find the pastor strolling toward him. He wore a white clerical collar, light blue shirt and black jacket, which seemed to enhance his fluffy white sideburns.

"That is one funny-looking dog," the pastor said in his deep, jovial voice.

"Don't tell Rags that. He thinks he's a pretty good-looking fellow."

"Ah, a suitably male self-perception." The pastor extended his hand. "Robert Walker. New in town?"

"Nick Carbini. Just passing through." As they shook hands, Nick noticed the preacher wore the silver Latin cross insignia of a military chaplain on his collar.

"Been out of the army long?"

The chaplain's question startled Nick and struck an uncomfortable chord. How had he known? "Four years, sir." He stood a little straighter.

"Just so you know I'm not a mind reader, Ward Cummings, who was greeting visitors this morning, mentioned there was a new vet in town."

"We met briefly at the barbershop in town," Nick admitted.

"Good man, Ward. I met him first in Iraq. He'd seen a lot of action there."

"Yes, sir." *The preacher had served in-country in Iraq?*

Glancing around, Nick tried to figure out how to make a hasty escape. Chaplain or not, he didn't want to talk about the war. Particularly not his service in Afghanistan or what had happened to him there.

"I spend a couple of days a month at the VA outpatient clinic in Kalispell. If you're looking for assistance to land a job or need some help with anything, there are good people there to give you a hand."

"I'll keep that in mind, sir." He released Rags from his leash and picked up the dog's water bowl and the throw rug.

"I'd better let you go, Carbini. Not talk your head off like my wife says I have a tendency to do." He chuckled at himself. "If you're still in town next Sunday, hope to see you in the congregation again."

"I'll try, sir."

Pastor Walker handed Nick a business card. "Call if you want to talk. Anytime." He turned and walked back toward the church entrance.

Nick jammed his card into his pocket, opened the truck door, and Rags jumped inside. Only when Nick got behind the wheel did he realize his hands were shaking and cold sweat beaded his forehead.

Had the pastor noticed that? Had he seen through Nick and knew about his nightmares and flashbacks? And that's why he suggested the VA clinic. So far the VA hadn't done much for him. The prison chaplain at least had tried.

Determined not to succumb to his fears, Nick

cranked the ignition and pulled a U-turn right in the middle of the church parking lot. He'd take a look around town, then get back to the diner where no one knew about the images that tormented him.

# *Chapter Six*

Back at the diner, Alisa hurried upstairs to change clothes. The Sunday morning brunch crowd was already beginning to fill the main room, and she'd soon be seating people in the room they used for private parties in the back.

She stuck her head into Mama's bedroom and found her sitting in her rocking chair by the window.

"How are you feeling?" she asked.

"I'm just bone weary, but I'll be fine by dinnertime."

"Rest as much as you need to, Mama. We'll take care of everything." Alisa began unzipping her dress. "Looks like we'll have a good brunch crowd. I'll be downstairs if you need me."

Mama waved her off. Slipping off her dress as she went to her room, Alisa worried about her mother. Usually Mama was like a storehouse of energy. No matter how hard she worked, Mama's energy didn't flag. Alisa wondered if it was time to get Mama to the doctor for a checkup, a challenging task at best.

After changing, she went downstairs, where Dotty and Tricia were all but galloping to keep up with the orders from a nearly full house. Alisa pitched in, seating guests as they arrived, giving them their menus, bringing them water and refilling coffee mugs. A good percentage of the patrons were locals she knew, so she exchanged pleasantries, checked up on their children and generally tried to make them feel at home.

Ward Cummings, his wife Betty Ann and his two teenage sons arrived, as promised.

"No need for menus," he said as she seated them at a table in the back room. "We're all having those potato pancakes you promised to save for us."

"I have them on special reserve just for you folks. I'll let your waitress know."

Smiling, she went to the fountain to get them their waters. After three tours of duty, Ward had been pretty messed up when he returned from Iraq. According to Betty Ann, who had confided in Alisa, Ward had had nightmares and anger issues. But Betty Ann had stuck with him. Over time, things had simmered down, and Ward had gotten his life back together.

To Betty's great relief. She'd once said some war wounds were harder to heal than others.

She carried a fresh pot of coffee to Henry Stephenson's table. Henry owned and operated Bear Lake Outfitters, a business that offered trail rides into the nearby wilderness area. A grandfather, he and his late wife had practically raised their grandson Bryan by themselves. Sitting with them was Jay Red Elk, Henry's wrangler who handled most of the trail rides these days.

She refilled their coffee mugs. "How's the outfitting business these days?"

"Jay's got a bunch of hunters he's leading out tomorrow," Henry said. "If he can keep 'em sober, they ought to bring back a deer or two."

"They'll stay sober," Jay said with a shake of his head. A big man, the hint of his Blackfeet heritage was evident in his prominent cheekbones. In contrast, his blue-green eyes had no doubt been inherited from a different branch of the family. "I'm not planning to hang around with any man who's been drinking and has a gun in his hands."

Alisa thought that was a smart decision on the part of the dark-haired guide.

"Enjoy your pancakes," she said to Bryan. As usual his mother was nowhere in sight. Krissy Stephenson seemed to have little time for the boy, which was a shame. About three years older than her Greg, Bryan was a good kid.

Some single moms didn't know what they were missing.

* * *

Nick parked his truck across the street from the house where he'd lived as a kid.

Not much more than a clapboard cottage, a thin thread of smoke drifted up from the chimney. A toddler's swing hung from the branch of a gnarly pine tree, and a stroller sat on the front porch. The gate on the picket fence across the front of the yard had long since been broken.

His throat tightened as he remembered living in that house. He pictured his father sitting in the old recliner downing a can of beer, the third or fourth that day. His voice loud and angry, complaining that dinner wasn't ready. His mother's hurried footsteps on the worn linoleum in the kitchen, the sound of pans clanking on the stove, her soft voice, "It'll be ready in a minute, Sam."

Tears burned at the back of his eyes. After all these years he remembered the sweetness of her voice. Her quiet laughter when they made pasta sauce from scratch. And her bleak eyes as she lost her battle with cancer.

His chin quivered. "I've missed you, Mom," he whispered to himself. So many years moving from place to place with his dad, and he'd missed his mother every single day. Still did.

Rags shifted in the backseat and poked his nose over Nick's shoulder, nuzzling his neck.

"I'm okay, boy. I'm okay."

He hooked his arm under the dog's neck, and gave him a few scratches under his chin. Looking across the road again, Nick rubbed his eyes with the heels of his hands. He cleared the painful lump in his throat.

Shifting into Drive, he pulled onto the narrow road and drove away.

He took the road that circled the lake. Out on the water, two water skiers in wet suits cut back and forth in the wake of their speedboat. Near the opposite shore, a couple of sailboats moved gracefully in a light breeze. Families sat on their private docks, smoke from barbecues drifted on the same breeze. Kids stood with fishing poles, their lines in the water.

None of those experiences had been Nick's as a kid. No boat rides or barbecues. No fishing except with an old stick and some line he'd found tangled in the bushes. He'd never caught a thing.

Idly he wondered if Alisa knew how to fish, and he smiled to himself imagining her in chest-high waders. That would be quite a sight to see.

During a late afternoon lull in customers in the diner, Alisa was behind the counter rolling place settings in napkins when Nick strolled in. There wasn't much pep in his step. His shoulders slumped. His eyes looked tired with more than a hint of melancholy.

Her chest filled with empathy. His afternoon hadn't been a happy one.

"Hi," she said with a brightness she hoped might dispel his mood. "Just coffee? Or are you hungry?"

Still wearing his white shirt with the sleeves rolled up and the good jeans he'd worn to church, he slid onto a stool. "Coffee first. Then I'll try one of your famous buffalo burgers."

"One black coffee comin' up." She plucked a mug off the stack and grabbed the coffeepot. "You found your way around town all right?"

"Yeah." He watched as she poured his coffee.

"It's changed some since you were here. The municipal park and dock are new. We have some nice festivals there during the summer. Country-and-western music. Art shows. Folk dancing exhibitions. They bring in quite a few tourists, which is good for business."

"Uh-huh." Without looking up, he wrapped his hands around the mug as if he was chilled to the bone.

She set the pot on the counter. "Guess driving around brought back some memories, huh?"

"Yeah." He looked up. "Some good. Some not so good."

Instinctively, to let him know she cared and understood, she touched his arm, her fingers brushing the scattering of dark hair on his forearm. She sensed the strength lying beneath the rigid feel of his flesh, the flex of well-honed muscles.

"I'm sorry," she whispered.

He covered her hand with his, sending ripples of warmth up her arm. He held her gaze. His amazing blue eyes filled with gratitude. "Thanks. I'm okay."

For a moment, she couldn't move. Couldn't turn away. Could barely breathe.

Laughter from the other end of the diner broke the spell.

She pulled her hand back and took a breath. "So, do you want fries with your burger?"

"Sure. I skipped lunch. I'm starved."

Picking up the coffeepot, she returned it to the warmer and fled to the kitchen to place his order. She should not be reacting to him so strongly. Not to the way his eyes had held hers. Or to the touch of his hand on hers. It meant nothing. He wouldn't be staying long. His sad memories of Bear Lake would most likely drive him away.

She was briefly distracted by Hector, who wanted to be sure she knew they were running low on potatoes, fresh squash and bagged salads. She assured him that Mama had placed a produce order, which would arrive tomorrow.

By the time she returned to the front of the diner, Nick's order was ready to pick up.

Nick, however, wasn't sitting at the counter.

Frowning, she glanced around and spotted him standing at the ol' duffers' booth, which was otherwise unoccupied except for the sign that said Reserved.

"Nick, your burger is ready," she called.

He turned. "What's with the jigsaw puzzle?"

"Some of our regulars like to work on it when they drop in."

"Can anyone give it a shot?"

She shrugged. None of the old timers were around, so why not? "Sure. You want to eat there?"

"Yeah, that'd be great."

She picked up his silverware and coffee mug, and carried them and his burger plate to the booth. Nick slid onto the pink vinyl seat. She put his order down in front of him.

"Is your mother okay now?"

"She took a nap this afternoon. Sometimes she gets extra tired, which worries me. She's not getting any younger, but she insisted she's fine to work the evening shift."

"You both work too hard." He plucked a French fry from his plate and popped it in his mouth.

"Our profit margin is pretty slim. Not enough there to hire another cook. Or waitress, for that matter."

"Making a restaurant profitable is a hard art to learn." He took a large bite of burger and nodded his approval. "Do you do jigsaw puzzles yourself?"

"I've been known to do a few. Winters can get pretty long around here."

"Hmm." He gestured to the seat opposite him. "Have you got time to sit awhile?"

His unexpected invitation took her by surprise. So much so, she sat without giving it much thought, although she knew she should have. "For a few minutes. Customer traffic will pick up in a bit."

Nodding with his mouth full of burger, he wiped his fingertips on a napkin. Eyeing the puzzle and the remaining pieces, he selected one with two bulges and dropped it into place.

"You're good," she said.

"Comes from having too much time on my hands." He grabbed the ketchup bottle and poured a generous amount over his fries. "Your turn." He tilted his head toward the puzzle.

Her brows rose. As it happened, she'd already spotted a piece that would fill the empty hole in the tree leaning over the bubbling brook. She eased it gently into place.

"Nice." Another bite of burger, a moment to study the puzzle, and he slipped a whimsically shaped jigsaw tile into its spot. He grinned, the light of challenge in his eyes.

"You think I can't keep up?" she asked.

"I'm sure you can," he said easily but with a trace of "show me" in his voice.

And so she did. She'd never thought of putting

a jigsaw puzzle together as a competitive event. But she rose to the occasion. Back and forth they went, taking turns.

She groaned when he selected a piece she'd had in mind. She saved her turn by finding another piece that worked.

He muttered under his breath when his next piece wouldn't fit, and she got two turns in a row.

Alisa got so tickled at the fierce way he concentrated, a grin built from inside out. "I'm one ahead of you, you know."

"I know. But not for long."

She was matching him piece for piece when Greg came running into the diner. His jacket had slipped off one shoulder and his shirt was hanging out of his pants.

"Mom! I saw Rags outside and I thought—" He skidded to a stop at the table. "Hi, Nick. I was hoping you'd be in here."

"Hey, sport. You found me, all right. What's up?"

"I figured if you were eating 'n stuff, you might like me to take Rags for a walk or play fetch with him or something."

Nick glanced to Alisa for her approval, which she appreciated. "It's fine with me. Just stay close, okay? It'll be time for your supper soon."

With no need for more encouragement, her son raced back out of the diner.

Reluctantly, she fingered another puzzle piece then slid it aside. "I'd better get back to work. The place is filling up."

He looked around as though he'd been unaware of the customers who had arrived while they'd been playing their game. "You'll give me another chance to beat you?"

Annoying heat rose to her cheeks. It wasn't like he was asking her on a date. Or even flirting with her.

"Sure." She stood. "Another time. As long as you don't mind losing."

His scowl made her laugh as she walked away.

Without much to do after he finished eating, Nick went back to his room. He stretched out on the comfortable queen-size bed, propped a pillow behind his head and switched on the television. He tuned into Sunday night football, but it didn't hold his attention.

Instead his mind kept replaying the way the tip of Alisa's tongue peeked out when she concentrated, searching for just the right puzzle piece. How tiny furrows formed a vee between her brows as she studied the puzzle. The way she tucked a wayward strand of blond hair behind her ear when it escaped from her ponytail, her fingers slender and graceful.

But most of all he replayed the feminine challenge in the tilt of her lips as she left him to take care of the newly arriving customers.

The woman was a tease. And a temptation. Neither of which he needed.

He snapped off the TV. "Come on, Rags. I know it's early, but it's time to clear my mind. If I don't, thinking about Alisa is going to keep me awake all night." Which would be a nice break from nightmares and flashbacks, now that he thought about it.

With Rags trotting beside him, Nick walked back behind the motel where he'd set up his chinning bar. The sun cast long shadows as it dipped toward the western horizon and the air was beginning to cool to a crisp autumn evening. The sound of dishes and conversation and the smell of grilling meat from the diner kitchen, barely reached him.

He lifted his arms and gripped the bar. His fingers curled on the familiar shape. He tightened his muscles.

His mind empty, he pulled and lowered himself in an easy rhythm until a new awareness crept up on him. He didn't know if it was her floral scent or if she'd made a sound, but he knew Alisa had walked up behind him.

Every muscle in his body tensed. *So much for emptying his mind.*

"So are you ready for your first lesson?" he asked without turning around.

Her shoes crushed dried leaves as she came closer. “Does it really help you sleep?”

“Most nights.” At least for a few hours.

Rags deserted him to greet Alisa.

“I don’t think I’ve got enough arm strength to pull myself up.”

He dropped to the ground. “You’d be surprised how strong you are. Come stand beside me. I’ll show you.”

“I know I couldn’t do chin-ups in high school. I doubt I’ve gotten any better.” The long rays of sunlight gleamed off of her hair casting the blonde strands in a red glow.

Nick swallowed hard. “Stand with your legs about shoulder wide then jump up to grab the bar.”

She tried to jump but failed to grasp it.

“Here. Let me help you.” He put his hands on her slender waist. “Okay, now jump.” He lifted her so she could grasp the rod. “There you go. Get a good grip. Now pull up.”

“Right.” She struggled but not well enough to get her chin over the bar. “You’re sure this will relax me?” she gasped.

His lips twitched. “It takes time to build up your strength.” With Alisa so close, his mind was far from empty. In fact, it was pretty busy admiring her.

“Okay, relax. Let’s try that again,” he said.

She relaxed her arms. He circled her waist again, ready to help her up just as she let go of the bar.

"Oh!" she cried.

He caught her and slowly lowered her to her feet. Now they were closer than ever, him holding her around the waist, her gazing into his eyes. Their faces mere inches apart. She licked her lips, leaving them glistening.

He knew he shouldn't. But he couldn't resist. Just this one time.

Leaning forward, he brought his lips to hers. The jolt of awareness, of her slight gasp of surprise, nearly undid him. He lingered a moment. Tasting her. Chiding himself for his weakness. For never wanting to let her go.

A scream ripped through the air.

They broke apart.

Eyes wide, for an instant Alisa froze. Another scream from the diner released her from her paralysis.

"That's Mama!" she cried.

Whirling, she sprinted for the kitchen door.

Nick's adrenaline surged. Without any thought but to help Mama, he was right on Alisa's heels. They went up the steps together. Nick reached for the door ahead of her and flung it open.

## *Chapter Seven*

Nick took in the scene at a glance. Hector and his helper shouting orders that no one heard. The smell of hot cooking oil. Mama on the floor, screaming. Her hands and forearms scalded red. The big deep-fry pot next to her, the over-heated contents spreading across the floor in an oily, slippery mess. Alisa on her knees trying to quiet her mother.

Nick squatted beside Mama. "Are you hurt anywhere besides your arms?"

"Dear Lord in heaven," she prayed. "Please stop it from hurting." Tears streamed down her cheeks.

"Mama, look at me." He turned her face toward him. "I need to move you out of the oil. Are you hurt anywhere else? Any broken bones?"

She shook her head.

Carefully, he slipped his arms beneath her shoulders and under her knees. "Alisa, grab some clean tablecloths and spread them out away from the stove."

As she hopped up to do as he'd asked, Nick lifted Mama, who let out another scream. "You're going to be all right, Mama. I promise. Just stay with me here. Stay with me. Keep nice and calm." As if with those burns, anyone could keep calm.

Nick turned to Hector, who was uselessly wringing his hands. "It was not my fault," Hector whined. "I didn't see anything and all of a sudden Mama was on the floor screaming."

"It doesn't matter, Hector. No one's blaming you. Get me some clean white cloths," he ordered. "Soak them in sterile water."

"But I—"

"Now, Hector!"

The cook fled, and Nick carried Mama to the tablecloths Alisa had spread on the floor.

Mama started to writhe.

"Try to stay still, Mama. We'll get you help in a minute." Nick caught Alisa's eye. "Call 9-1-1."

She blinked. "Of course. I wasn't thinking." She pulled her cell phone from her pocket and stepped away.

Nick tried to get a good look at the burns on Mama's arms and hands. Solid red in color. Some blistering. At least second-degree burns, he was sure. He'd seen a few kitchen injuries like that before. Had to hurt like blazes. The hands especially. The tender skin between her fingers.

Hector arrived with an armload of wet dish towels.

"That's good. Hand them to me one at a time." He bent close to Mama. "I'm going to wrap your arms loosely with these towels. They'll cool the burns until we can get you to the hospital."

He glanced up to see Jolene, one of the regular waitresses, standing inside the swinging doorway between the kitchen and the front of the diner. She was holding back a red-faced, frightened Greg with her arms around him.

"Mama's going to be all right," Nick called to the boy. She wouldn't be all right anytime soon, but he was sure she would recover. Likely she'd be scarred.

Carefully, using one towel at a time, he wrapped her arms and looped the towels around her hands.

Alisa knelt across from him and soothed her mother's forehead. "Ambulance will be here soon."

"Good. How far away is the hospital?" Nick asked.

"Bear Lake Medical Clinic is about five minutes away. Our EMTs are part of the volunteer fire department. Sometimes, if they're off somewhere, it takes them a while to answer the call."

Nicked prayed they'd get here soon.

The cool towels seemed to ease some of Mama's

pain. She drew a shuddering breath and looked up at Alisa. "I don't know what happened. I reached for the deep fryer and then—"

"Sh, Mama," Alisa said. "Don't worry about that now."

"Don't let anyone slip—"

"Hector's already cleaning up the hot oil." Alisa stroked her mother's hair back from her forehead.

"What about our customers? People are waiting—"

"We'll find a way to take care of them. Don't worry, Mama," Alisa said, although she didn't look entirely convinced herself.

Sitting back on his haunches, Nick took a good look around. The staff looked flummoxed. They needed someone to take control. Alisa's face was nearly as white as the damp cloths around her mother's arms. She was in no condition to handle the kitchen and waitstaff. She needed to be with her mother.

Amid clatter and heavy footsteps, the EMTs arrived via the back door. Both of them looked to be in their mid-thirties and moved with confidence.

Relieved they had arrived so quickly, Nick backed out of the way as one EMT knelt beside Mama, put a cuff on her arm above the wrapped cloth to take her blood pressure and pulse. The other arranged the gurney and set up a heart monitor.

"She has second-degree burns from hot oil over

both of her arms up to her elbows," Nick told the two men. "I don't know if oil splashed on her anywhere else."

Nodding his understanding, the first EMT spoke quietly. "Well, now, Mama. You weren't supposed to be cooking yourself for supper."

"Silly me," she whispered and shivered. Chances were good she was going into shock.

The second guy covered her with a blanket. "Okay, Mama. We're going to get you onto the gurney then we'll pay a visit to Doc Jo at the clinic. He'll take good care of you."

Standing off to the side, Alisa had the look of an accident victim. Pale face. Wide eyes. In shock. "I want to go with Mama to the hospital. But who's going to take care of the diner? Our customers? Hector can't. And Greg—"

"I'll take charge of the kitchen," Nick said.

Greg escaped from Jolene's grasp. "Mom, I want to go with you and Mama."

"Oh, honey, you can't—"

Stepping forward, Nick hooked his hand over the boy's shoulder. "It would really help your mom, son, if you'd stay here with Jolene. You could take care of the customers out front, bring 'em water and clear away the plates. Can you do that?"

His blue eyes darted from Nick to his mother.

With a quick glance toward her mother on the gurney, Alisa knelt in front of her son. "Nick's right. You'd be a big help here at the diner. Jolene needs you because she's going to be in charge out front. I'll look after Mama and tell you about it when I get home."

The boy managed an uneasy nod as his chin trembled.

"We'd better get hustling, kiddo," Jolene said. "We don't want unhappy customers, do we?"

Alisa gave him a quick kiss and urged him toward Jolene. "I love you."

As soon as Greg turned away, Nick took Alisa's arm. "Ride in the ambulance with Mama. You're in no shape to drive. I'll take care of things here and come to the clinic later to check on you and Mama."

"Are you sure?"

"Go," he insisted.

Once she was out the door, he turned around to check on the cook staff. Only then did he become aware of the stainless steel appliances and prep tables all around him. The reflections that splintered images into prisms of dark, shattering pain.

He squeezed his eyes closed and reached for the rubber ball in his pocket. *Not now! You can't let go. It's only your imagination. Like a dream. It can't hurt you. It's only playing tricks on your brain. What you're seeing happened years ago.*

Cautiously, he opened his eyes. Hector and the helper were staring at him. Nick couldn't just stand there like a frozen ice sculpture starting to melt. He had to keep his flashbacks at bay. Somehow.

"Okay, let's get back on track." His voice was rusty and scratchy in his throat. "What orders do we have waiting, Hector?"

Fortunately, most kitchens worked the same way. A row of orders lined up in front of the cooks. Cold food like meat and eggs stored near the prep tables. Bread and rolls nearby that the waitstaff added to the plates.

He heard Rags whining at the door. He stepped outside and drew a deep breath. "Good boy. You stay right there, okay? I'll come get you when I can."

The dog whined again, then laid down on the porch. He made one effort to wag his tail before resting his head on his paws.

Trying to keep his head empty of anything except the job at hand, Nick went back into the kitchen. He helped Hector catch up on the orders. Burgers and fries. Roasted half chicken, mashed potatoes and gravy. T-bone medium rare with a side salad.

When everything seemed to be running smoothly again, he walked out front. The place wasn't crowded, which was a blessing.

"How's it going?" he asked Jolene.

"We're okay. I put the Closed sign on the door and switched off the Open sign. We close early on Sunday night anyway. And to make up for the slow service, I'm giving everyone free coffee or sodas, whatever they want."

"Sounds good."

"They're all as worried about Mama as I am," Jolene added, her forehead furrowed. "She's an institution around here."

"I know." He was worried too, not about her survival—the burns didn't look fatal—but her recovery, which would be long and painful. "How's your new helper?" he asked as Greg came by with two dirty plates in his hands. He dumped them in the tub with the other dirty dishes.

"He's great." Jolene winked at the boy. "I think Mama ought to hire him full-time."

"Yeah! Then I wouldn't have to go to school."

Nick ruffled his hair. "Don't think your mother will go for that, sport. But nice try."

With an easy shrug, Greg went back to work.

"How bad is Mama?" Jolene asked softly.

"She's going to be out of action for a while."

Jolene grimaced. "That's going to put a big burden on Alisa. She'll have to hire a new cook. Where she'll find a decent cook on short notice is beyond me. As it is, we already run on a pretty skimpy staff."

A bare bones staff, Nick agreed, and a narrow profit margin. Losing Mama for a few weeks sounded like a ready-made opportunity for disaster to strike.

But how could he, terrified of the images he might see in the shiny stainless steel, risk having a full-fledged, cringing-on-the-floor meltdown that would reveal his darkest secret?

It was almost ten when Nick made his way to the small Bear Lake Medical Clinic, a modern two-story building with a red neon sign identifying the emergency entrance. He parked in the nearly empty lot, left Rags in the truck and went into the waiting area.

Only one elderly man sat dozing in one of the turquoise chairs.

Nick walked over to the receptionist. "I'm looking for Alisa Machak. Her mother was brought in a few hours ago?"

The middle-aged woman looked up at him over the top of her half-glasses. "They're getting ready to take Mama Machak up to her room. I think Alisa went to the chapel. It's around the corner across from the gift shop."

"Thanks." Following the woman's directions, he found the door standing open to the small chapel. Alisa sat on a pew facing a tranquil mountain scene. Soft music played in the background.

Tentative about disturbing her thoughts and prayers, he called quietly, "Alisa?"

She turned, spotting him. Immediately, she was on her feet running toward him. He opened his arms to catch and hold her. He rubbed his hand up and down her back as she sobbed, and soothed his palm over her soft, silken hair, inhaling the fresh fruity scent of her shampoo. All the while he told himself he should let her go. He shouldn't hold her like this, not so close. But he couldn't release her, not when she needed to be held. Even a strong woman needed someone to lean on once in a while.

"Poor Mama," she cried. "She was in so much pain. There was nothing I could do. Nothing." Her breath caught.

"I'm sure the doctor's doing whatever he can for her."

"I know. It's just so hard to see her like that."

He wanted to brush a kiss to her temple. Just to reassure her, he told himself, although he knew that was a lie. "The receptionist told me they're about to take her up to her room," he said.

She sniffed. "The doctor gave her a shot for her pain. And then they were going to take her upstairs. He said he'd come tell me when I can see her."

"Good. The shot will help her rest."

Still teary-eyed, she eased herself away. "Looks like I got your jacket all wet." She brushed her fingertips over the spot where her tears had fallen on his old khaki jacket.

"Don't worry. It'll dry."

She found a tissue in her pocket, dried her tears and blew her nose. "I'm not usually a crier."

"I know. Somebody who chops wood like you do has got to be tough." But on the inside, she was soft and caring with her son and mother. Her customers too. An attribute he admired.

The tiniest hint of a smile curved her lips. "How's everything at the diner?"

"It's good. We got everybody fed, and Jolene closed a little early. She's staying with Greg 'til you get back."

"Jolene is a gem. I don't know what I'd do without her."

Nick eased Alisa back to a pew. "Everyone is worried about Mama. She's an *institution* in Bear Lake, I'm told."

"She is that." Alisa sat down. She twisted the tissue in her hands. "I wish the doctor would come back."

"All in God's time." Unable to resist, Nick slipped his arm around her shoulders and gave her an encouraging squeeze.

Her brows rose. "God's time?"

"That's what my army lieutenant said when they dragged us off somewhere in a hurry, then we had to sit around and wait for what seemed like an eternity until whatever was going to happen, happened." The opposite was the case the day his outpost in Afghanistan was overrun. He and his crew had gone from business as usual to terror in a millisecond that lasted forever. That forever hadn't stopped yet for Nick. Not with the flashbacks and dreams that haunted him.

The doctor walked into the chapel. "Alisa."

"Dr. Johansen." She popped to her feet.

Nick stood. If the doctor hadn't been wearing a white jacket and a stethoscope draped around his neck, Nick would have taken him for a teenager who'd wandered into the wrong place. His jeans and expensive running shoes suggested he'd be right at home playing one-on-one basketball in a local park with his buddies.

"Your mother is all settled in her room now," he said. "You can go up to see her but I don't want you to stay long. She needs to rest."

The doctor turned his attention to Nick. "Were you the one who wrapped Mrs. Machak's arms?"

"I did, yes."

"Good job. You did the right thing."

He shrugged, uncomfortable with the doctor's praise. "They gave us a little first aid training when I was in the army. I just did what I was taught."

"How long do you think Mama will be in the hospital?" Alisa asked.

"A couple of days. Maybe more. The biggest concern now is pain management and infection. We'll see how it goes."

"How long do you think before she'd be able—"

"To get back to work?" the doctor asked. He shook his head. "Maybe six weeks. As she heals, she'll need some physical therapy for her hands. I wouldn't want her to rush that."

"No, of course not." Alisa sighed, which made Nick want to put his arm around her again. But he resisted. She'd been vulnerable when she'd let him hold her. He didn't want to push her. He had no right to push her.

"From what you told me in the E.R.," the doctor said, "I suspect Mama could use a nice, long rest anyway."

"I'll see that she gets it, Doctor. Thank you."

The doctor left, promising to keep Alisa updated on her mother's condition.

Nick and Alisa went upstairs.

The lights were dimmed in Mama's room. Her gray hair stood out on the stark white pillowcase and her eyes were closed. Her bandaged arms lay on top of the sheet that covered her.

Nick lingered by the door as Alisa approached the bed.

"Mama. Are you awake?"

Slowly, Mama's eyes opened and focused on her daughter. "My little princess. That's what your papa used to say." Her speech slurred the words together.

"I know, Mama. The doctor gave you something to help you sleep."

"What a silly goose I was. I should've known better. What will we do—?"

"Don't worry about anything. Nick and Jolene took care of everything at the diner. We'll be fine. You concentrate on healing and getting well."

Her mother gaze swung slowly to Nick in the doorway. "I told you he's a good man." Her eyes closed and she was asleep.

Alisa kissed her mother's forehead. "Sleep tight, Mama." She stepped away from the bed.

As she left the room, her head was bent, her steps slow. When they reached the stairs, she looked up at Nick. Tears glistened in her eyes.

"How in the world am I going to manage at the diner for six weeks without Mama?"

He slid his arm around her again. "I don't know, but you'll find a way."

Shaking her head, she walked down the stairs as though the weight of the world had landed on her shoulders.

He stayed at the top of the stairs. He could barely draw a breath, and it hurt when he tried. His palms started to sweat. His mouth went dry. The urge to run, to run as far away from Alisa and the diner as he could, drummed through his veins. Run from the images that leaped out from stainless steel prep counters and refrigerators. Stove tops and cooking pots.

He couldn't stay. He had to run.

Alisa needed him.

He had to tell her everything. Le Cordon Bleu. Prison.

But not right now when she was so upset about her mother.

"Wait!" His work boots clattered on the stairs as he ran down after her. "I can cook."

## *Chapter Eight*

Alisa whirled. "What did you say?"

Breathless, he halted in front of her. "I can cook. I'll fill in for your mother until she recovers."

"Nick, that's sweet of you to offer. You might be able to fry a burger, but we need a chef. Someone who knows how to plate a whole meal, not just fry an egg or two."

"Alisa, as soon as I graduated from high school, I enlisted in the army. I signed up to be a cook, and they sent me to school."

"Okay," she said tentatively while her blue eyes revealed only doubt. "Maybe you could help Hector."

He grasped her shoulders, forcing her to listen to him. "They sent me to Le Cordon Bleu in Paris. For a year. I can cook more than burgers and fries, and I can manage food service for two thousand or more hungry soldiers. I can help you."

Her jaw dropped open. "Two thousand?"

"Or I can serve forty command officers *tournedos sautés aux champignons* with baked tomatoes, artichoke hearts and potato balls sautéed in butter followed by cherry tart flambée." He relaxed his grip on her. "But spaghetti and meatballs are my specialty. That, my mother taught me."

Looking bewildered, she shook her head. "I had no idea."

"Yeah, well, I don't talk about it much." For very good reasons.

"Why in the world did the army send you to Le Cordon Bleu and then ship you to Afghanistan to cook for the troops?"

"I admit I'd expected to be assigned to an officers' club somewhere. Maybe even the Pentagon. I spent like a week at the army headquarters in Kabul, then they sent me to an isolated outpost. The army is full of surprises." He eased her toward the hospital's main entrance. "Let's get you home. You're going to need your rest. We'll talk about all this tomorrow."

In the time it took Nick to drive her back to the diner, Alisa still hadn't absorbed the fact that he was a trained chef. Far better trained that anyone she could hire locally. Far and above the training she had, which had all been on-the-job with her parents.

Her mind reeling, she walked upstairs to the family living quarters.

Why hadn't he mentioned that before? And why had he taken a job as a handyman instead of applying to be a cook? With that kind of training, he could be working at any number of upscale restaurants earning big bucks anywhere in the country. His talents would be wasted at a diner.

But then she remembered he was a drifter. He didn't want to settle down to a steady job. Didn't want to tie himself to responsibilities.

Nick wanted to wander around the country without any ties at all. Like Greg's father.

In the family quarters, Jolene was curled up on the couch with an afghan over her. The moment Alisa stepped into the room, she sat up. "How's Mama?"

Her body aching from too much stress, Alisa sat down on the arm of the couch. "The doctor gave her a pain shot. She was sleeping comfortably when I left."

"What's her prognosis?"

"Overall, it's good. But it will be weeks before she's ready to go back to work." Tears burned at the back of her eyes, and one leaked out. She thought she was all done crying.

"Oh, honey…" Jolene patted Alisa's hand. "I'm so sorry this happened."

"Me too."

"Mommy?" Dressed in his pajamas, Greg stood at his bedroom door.

Alisa held out her arms. "Come here, munchkin."

Her son ran across the room and into her arms. His messy hair smelled of little-boy sweat, and his body was warm from sleep. She relished the sturdy feel of his young, healthy body, the love he gave so unconditionally.

She slipped off the arm of the couch and onto the seat, and held him on her lap. He'd soon be too big to hold and cuddle. She'd miss that, she thought as she told him about Mama and how she'd be home in a few days.

"Can I visit her at the hospital?" he asked.

"Of course you may. I'll take you tomorrow. You can go in late to school." Somehow she'd find time after the breakfast rush to visit her mother. Then she'd need to start looking for a new waitress to hire. Put Jolene in charge of the front of the diner while she worked the kitchen.

While Nick cooked?

She shook her head, hardly believing he was a trained chef. *Le Cordon Bleu*! She almost laughed at that. A big strapping guy who could do fifty chin-ups without breaking a sweat was a French-trained chef.

With a quiet wave of her hand, Jolene mouthed goodbye and slipped out of the room.

Greg started to relax in her arms. His eyelids fluttered closed. She walked him into his bedroom, tucked him in. He rolled on to his side, asleep in an instant. She kissed him goodnight and whispered a prayer for her mother's recovery.

Back in the living room, she looked out the window toward the motel. The rooms were all dark, including Nick's. Only the exterior night lights remained on and dimmed.

She placed her palm on the cold window glass as though she could reach out and touch him. "Good night. Sleep tight."

Rising early the next morning, she hurried downstairs. She needn't have rushed. Nick had apparently helped himself to a white chef's jacket from the linen supply and had everything under control. He looked exceptionally handsome and totally at home standing in front of the stove, radiating self-confidence.

The scent of freshly baked cinnamon rolls filled the kitchen. Four blackberry pies were cooling on the counter, four apple pies baking in the oven. Nick was beating meringue for the banana pies that Mama usually prepared herself.

The rest of the kitchen staff were at their stations preparing to serve breakfast. She had no idea how Nick had managed to take over Mama's role so easily and quickly.

All that military experience, she thought with renewed astonishment.

Alisa strolled over to Nick. “You didn’t mention you could bake pies, too.”

His lips hitched into a grin as he spread meringue on the pie. “Courtesy of the U.S. Army, I’m afraid.”

“They look delicious.”

He cast her a sideways glance. “You want a slice for breakfast?”

“Don’t tempt me.”

She walked around the kitchen, assuring the helpers and dishwashers that Mama would be fine and return home soon.

“That Nick fella sure knows what he’s doing,” Betsy Holland, a kitchen helper who had worked the early shift for years, whispered. “Good-looking guy, too.” The older woman waggled her brows.

Alisa felt a rush of heat touch her cheeks. “We’re fortunate he’s an experienced chef.”

As she was about to leave the kitchen to check the front, Nick said, “When you have a few minutes, there’s something we need to talk about.”

“Sure.” A pay raise? Understandable. Or how soon he was planning to move on to somewhere else? She didn’t know what he might have on his mind. Whatever it was, she’d simply have to cope.

She found a nice crowd of customers eating breakfast. She grabbed a pot of coffee and made the rounds to help out the two waitresses working the morning shift.

Ezra Cummings at the ol' duffers' table stopped her. "What's all this about Mama being hurt?"

She quickly brought Ezra and his buddies up to date, then moved on to the next table of regulars. Everyone expressed their concern and sympathy. She imagined by noon Mama's hospital room would be overflowing with flowers. Like family, the folks of Bear Lake took care of their own.

When the crowd had thinned, Alisa returned to the kitchen.

"Things out front have slowed," she said to Nick. "Is this a good time to talk? I promised I'd take Greg to see Mama this morning."

"Now is fine." He spoke to Betsy about the unfilled orders, then shed his white jacket. "Let's step outside."

He held the door for her and followed her down the steps he'd repaired. The morning air felt crisp after the overheated kitchen. She wrapped her arms around herself.

Nick untied Rags, gave the dog a quick scratch behind his ears, then walked a few paces away from the building before stopping to take in a deep breath of fresh air. He turned toward her. The deep grooves lining his forehead were pulled into a frown.

"I didn't think it mattered when I was just doing

handyman work around the place," he said. "Now that I'm working inside..." He hooked his thumbs in the pockets of his jeans.

An uneasy feeling crept down Alisa's spine.

He blew out a breath and glanced up at the cloudless sky. "I spent the past three years in prison in Louisiana. Assault and battery."

Unable to speak, she gaped at him.

"I got into a barroom fight. Not the first time, either. I messed up the other guy pretty bad and sent him to the hospital, not that he hadn't thrown a few good punches my way. But that's no excuse for what I did."

"Were you drunk?"

"Yes. I've been clean and sober since that night when they locked me up. I don't drink anymore. I thought you should know."

*Should know?* Her son idolized Nick. A drunk with a temper. She never should have let Greg get so close to Nick.

She never should have shared a kiss with Nick.

Or wished there could have been more.

Unable to hold his gaze a moment longer, couldn't look into the depth of his sky-blue eyes, she stepped away and turned her back on him.

"I'll understand if you want me to leave." His voice was low and somehow filled with the same pain that blossomed in her chest.

"If I'd known—"

"You would have thrown me out. I understand. Now you've got a real problem with your mother out of commission for a while. I'll leave if you want me to. Or stay until you can find someone else or Mama is able to come back to work. Either way, I promise not a drop of alcohol will cross my lips. I won't do anything that will hurt you or your family or your business."

Alisa studied the ground around her feet. Pine needles and faded oak leaves lay scattered across the hard-packed dirt where feet had trampled the ground for decades. Machak feet. Their friends and customers.

How could Nick promise he wouldn't drink? How could she count on a few well-intentioned words to keep him sober? Keep him from losing his temper with the staff?

Or worse, lose his temper with her own son? Nick wasn't the sort of man a young, impressionable boy should have as a role model. Was he?

The kitchen door opened. "Mom, I ate my breakfast. Can we go see Mama now?"

Rags came running over to greet her son, who knelt to rough up the dog's shaggy coat.

Alisa swallowed hard. "In a minute, honey."

"Can I play with Rags 'til you're ready to go?"

"No!" The word came out too sharply. She glanced at Nick.

"Go ahead. Visit your mother. You can decide what you want to do about me later."

How could she possibly tell him to leave when she needed his help? And a stubborn part of her, a part that had been lonely too long, desperately wanted him to stay?

She didn't want to judge him for his past actions. After all she wasn't the same person she'd been when she got pregnant with Greg. With the help of the Lord, she'd changed. Surely Nick had too.

It was true that Nick scared her, but not because he'd been in jail. He scared her by what he made her feel.

Nick put Rags back on the leash that was tied to the stair railing. "Sorry, fella. I'll take a break this afternoon and let you run. Stay."

Rags lowered himself to the ground with an audible sigh.

Leaving his dog, Nick went into the kitchen. He figured he'd be smarter to go pack his things and get out of town. Alisa was sure to tell him to leave when she returned to the diner.

What woman wanted an ex-con working for her? Or hanging around her son? He'd seen the disbelief in her eyes turn to shock. And then a shadowed hint of fear before she looked away.

The last thing he'd ever do was hurt her or her

son. But she couldn't rely on the word of an ex-con and former drunk.

Prison had changed him. Mostly for the better because of Chaplain McDuff, who with the patience of Job had led him to the Lord.

But living with a bunch of hard-core inmates, some of them lifers, had changed Nick, too. He had an edge now, a wariness that made him keep others at arms' length. Between that and PTSD, he wasn't a prime candidate for any job. Or a relationship with a woman as caring and compassionate as Alisa.

Keeping his eyes averted from the reflections in the stainless steel prep tables and appliances, he grabbed a menu and sat down at a table in a back room set up for employees taking a break. He wanted to be sure he was familiar with the dinner choices and check to be sure nothing should be pulled from the menu because of lack of supplies.

Or lack of a cook who knew how to prepare the dish.

With his fingertips, he rubbed his temples against a threatening headache. By dinnertime he could be gone.

Alisa stopped at the door of Mama's hospital room, surprised to find Dr. Royce McCandless, Greg's pediatrician, at her mother's bedside.

Greg pushed right past Alisa. "Hey, Mama. How come Dr. McCandless is here? You're not a kid."

Mama smiled at her grandson, and the doctor drew Greg closer to the bed. A large bouquet of flowers stood on the nearby bed table.

"I'm visiting your grandmother as a friend, young man. Not as her doctor."

That seemed to satisfy Greg, who shifted his attention to Mama's bandaged arms. "Does it still hurt?" he asked her.

"A little bit." Mama lifted her gaze to Dr. McCandless. "Thank you for coming by."

In a casual gesture, the doctor stroked a loose strand of hair away from Mama's cheek. "I'll drop by later to see how you're doing."

Alisa told him goodbye, then moved to her mother's bedside opposite Greg. An IV dripped medication into Mama's arm. "How are you feeling this morning?"

"A little punchy. The medicine, it makes me not hurt but my head is swimming."

"Has Dr. Johansen been in to see you?"

Her nearly white eyebrows pulled together. "Earlier, I think. He said I was lucky. I won't have to have surgery."

That was a relief. But her mother still looked paler than usual and her eyes were unnaturally dilated. A reaction to the meds, Alisa assumed.

Turning to Greg, Mama said, "Why you're not in school this morning?"

"Mom said I could come see you first." His smooth forehead scrunched into a worried frown. "I was afraid you might die like grandpa did."

"Not me, my little *vnuk,"* she said, using the Czech word for *grandson*. "Your grandmama is too stubborn to die from such a little thing."

Greg climbed up the bed rail far enough to kiss her cheek. "I'm glad, Mama. I'd miss you a lot."

Her throat thickening with tears, Alisa saw a sheen form her in mother's eyes. "I would miss you, too, my little one." Mama's voice was laced with love.

"Greg, honey." Alisa cleared her throat. "Could you go downstairs and wait for me? I have some business I want to talk to Mama about for a minute. Then I'll take you to school."

"Okay." With an easy shrug, he hopped down and ambled out into the hallway.

"What is it? Did something go wrong? Someone else hurt themselves?"

"No, Mama, nothing like that." Taking a deep breath, Alisa forced herself to continue. "Last night, after we saw you, Nick told me something I didn't expect. He's an experienced, trained chef."

"Ah, that is a good thing, yes? He can help you until I get better."

"He could, yes." Alisa hesitated. She didn't want

to worry her mother. But she was so conflicted about Nick, her feelings for him and her fears about him, that she needed Mama's advice. "This morning he told me he is an ex-convict. He spent three years in prison for hurting another man."

Mama's pale eyes widened. "That does not sound like the Nick I know."

"It's true. He was drunk and got into a fight."

"Have you seen him drink since he's been here? Or smelled alcohol on his breath?"

Her heart squeezed as she remember the sweet taste of his kiss. "No," she whispered. "He says he doesn't drink anymore."

Mama nodded. "Good for him. If that is true, why do you look so worried?"

"Didn't you say his father was a heavy drinker?"

"That doesn't mean Nick will be the same."

"I don't know. I mean, what if he starts drinking again? I can't have him around Greg. Or the staff." Nor did she want to be around him if he started drinking again. "I know with you unable to work, we need help in the kitchen. But maybe I could hire someone. There has to be—"

"Alisa! What do they say about not buying trouble?" Mama touched her bandaged hand to Alisa's, which was wrapped tightly around the bed rail. "Is it not possible that God has led Nick to us for a reason?"

"We don't know that, Mama."

"Give the man a chance, *Alisova.* Men can change, you know. I believe Nick already has."

Alisa wanted to believe that. But did she dare?

# *Chapter Nine*

Since Nick had told Alisa two days ago that he was an ex-con, she'd been avoiding him. Sure she'd helped out in the kitchen when they got rushed. Checked with him about what to order from the wholesaler. But she hadn't spoken a word about anything that wasn't work-related.

And she'd kept Greg away from him and Rags.

But she hadn't told him to get lost.

He glanced up at the wall clock. Almost seven. Based on the number of orders he and Hector had plated, the Wednesday night crowd must be light. This might be a good time to check on the veterans that met at the barbershop.

Taking off his white jacket, he hung it on a hook and went in search of Alisa.

Jolene was working the front tables. Only a couple were occupied. Two guys were eating at the counter.

"Is Alisa around?" he asked as Jolene returned to the coffee station.

"We aren't very busy, so she went upstairs to be with Greg. Go on up. Just knock on the door. It isn't Greg's bedtime yet."

"Thanks." He glanced up the stairs wondering what kind of a reception he'd get by invading her privacy. Whatever, he thought with a shrug. He couldn't leave without telling her. Besides, he'd been curious about where she lived and wanted to picture her there at the end of the day.

He climbed the stairs and rapped his knuckles on the door.

"Come in," she called.

He ran his fingers through his hair to tame the natural waves that had their own mind, opened the door and stepped inside.

Greg was sprawled on the floor in front of a forty-inch TV screen in the living room, which was comfortably furnished with a couch, swivel rocker and a recliner. Alisa sat at a small maple kitchen table working a jigsaw puzzle. He smiled, remembering their challenge.

"Hi. It's me."

Alisa's head snapped up. She shoved her chair back, toppling it over as she stood. "Oh. I thought you were Jolene." Her blond hair hung loose around her shoulders in a shimmer of molten honey.

"Sorry to disappoint."

"Hey, Nick," Greg called. "I'm watching a good show. You wanna watch with me?"

"Maybe another time, sport."

Her face flushed, Alisa straightened the chair she'd knocked over. She gripped the back of it as if she expected the chair to throw itself to the ground again. Or she was using the chair as a shield. "Is there something you wanted?"

"Yeah. Business is pretty light. There's some-place I want to go. I think Hector can handle things 'til closing."

"Oh. All right." She relaxed her grip enough to let the blood flow back to her knuckles. "I was going to come down in a bit to talk to you. Mama insists she's coming home tomorrow."

"Okay." Did that mean Alisa wanted him gone by then? He glanced toward the large window in the living room, which had a clear view of the motel. The outside security lights illuminated the geraniums in the flower box.

"I'm not sure the doctor will actually release her. But if I know Mama, she'll walk out on her own if she has to."

"I wouldn't doubt that for a minute." He'd grown fond of Mama. She had a warrior's spirit that would never give up. He suspected Alisa had in-herited the same determination.

"She won't be able to do any work. Her hands

are still bandaged. But she wants to teach you how to make her chicken and dumplings Czech style."

"Yeah?" He grinned. A new recipe, particularly one that tasted as great as Mama's chicken and dumplings, was always a treat to try. "That'd be great. I figured out some of the spices when I ate the dish. But the proportions are always tricky."

"Mama was afraid we'd have to scratch the special if she wasn't around. It's always a big night for us."

"I know. I saw the crowd last week." Had it only been a week since he arrived in Bear Lake? It felt longer. Almost as if his staying was a permanent thing. He wasn't counting on that. His nightmares may have ebbed, but that could be temporary.

"So, ah, have a good time tonight," Alisa said.

"Just out with the guys at the barbershop."

She tensed again. "I'll see you in the morning."

"Right." Hating the look of distrust in her eyes, he took a step backward. Did she think he was going out to get drunk and take a swing at someone?

"See ya, Nick." Greg waved but didn't look away from the TV.

"'Night, Greg." He nodded to Alisa. "See you tomorrow."

Descending the stairs, he muttered to himself. "What'd you think she'd do after you told her you were an ex-con? Jump into your arms? Tell you it didn't matter? Kiss you again?"

*Not gonna happen, Carbini. She's scared to death that you'll fall off the wagon. Or do something else crazy. Like when your old man knocked you and your mother around when he got drunk. Which was pretty much all the time.*

Nick untied Rags and started for the barbershop.

*Please, God, don't let me be like my dad. Not ever.*

"Hey, Carbini!" At the barbershop, Ned Turner greeted Nick with an extended hand and a slap on the back. "Come on in the back room. Mac's wife made us chocolate chip cookies."

"Great. Can my dog come?"

"Sure. Bring him in."

A half dozen guys were sitting around in a circle drinking coffee. The plate of cookies on the table was almost empty.

Nick recognized Ward and Mitchell from the day he had his hair cut, and was introduced to the others. Tony, who had the build of a Special Ops guy, had been back in town for less than a week. The way his dark eyes darted around the room, Nick was pretty sure he hadn't settled into civilian life yet. He was due for another tour in less than a month.

Nick poured himself a mug of coffee and grabbed one of the last cookies.

He sat in one of the folding chairs and glanced around the room. A couple of posters of Glacier National Park hung on the wall and two fishing poles were mounted above a stuffed trout that had to have weighed twenty pounds.

The guys were telling tales of their military exploits. Most of them pretty hairy and probably exaggerated like when a fisherman claims to have caught the biggest fish on record—except it got away. Even so, beneath their laughter was a layer of truth that they all recognized. Things happened in a war that could never be forgotten.

Ward turned to Nick. "How'd you earn your sergeant stripes?"

"By cooking up the best mess of spaghetti and meatballs ever eaten in Afghanistan." That was the pat answer he usually gave anyone who asked. They laughed, as expected.

"Sounds like tough duty," Mac commented, chuckling.

Nick sipped his coffee. "Yeah, it was. I still get flashbacks."

"You mean indigestion?" Mac barked another laugh.

"Yeah, pretty much the same thing, isn't it?" Nick had discovered most veterans couldn't grasp the possibility that a cook, a noncombatant, could suffer from PTSD. One VA counselor had all but scoffed at him. Civilians didn't get it at all. He'd pretty much given up trying to convince anyone he had a problem. He'd deal with it himself.

The group quieted. Ned walked over to Nick and gave his shoulder a reassuring squeeze. "We've all been there, son. It gets better with time."

Nick sure hoped so. This past week hadn't been too bad. Rags had woken him a couple of times in the middle of a dream before the nightmare could rip him screaming from his sleep. The rest of the time he'd slept through the night. Practically a record for him.

Ward leaned toward Nick. "There's help for you if you need it."

Shrugging, Nick shook his head. "I'm doing better," he lied.

The attention moved away from him, shifting to good-natured insults among the guys. Nick began to relax until he remembered the distrustful look in Alisa's eyes when he'd said he'd see her in the morning.

She might be right not to trust him. But it still hurt deep in his gut. That wasn't something he knew how to change.

Alisa wandered over to the living room window. It was practically ten o'clock. She should be asleep.

Work started early at the Pine Tree Diner. But she was too restless to even lie down.

Despite her best efforts, she couldn't get Nick out of her mind. Why had he gotten into a fight? One so violent he'd hurt a man badly enough that he'd been sent to jail?

In the week Nick had been here, she'd only seen his gentle side. Not a trace of anger or violence. He'd been that way as a boy, too. Was it alcohol that had made him change? Or living with a drunken father?

She looked across at the motel. Nick's room was dark. Was he still out with the guys at the barbershop? *Drinking?* Would he come to work in the morning hungover?

Her gaze drifted to the back of the motel. There, in the dim night lights, she saw Nick's shadowed image doing chin-ups on the bar he'd stuck between two trees. The way he worked out so hard, it was like he was driven by some inner affliction. Something on the inside that he needed to vanquish.

Mama had told her to give Nick a chance. It was one thing to have him working in the kitchen. But did she dare risk her heart on such a troubled man?

"I don't need a wheelchair. It's my hands and arms that were burned." Mama held up her bandaged limbs for the hospital volunteer to see. "There's nothing wrong with my own two feet."

"Mama, please." Alisa had brought her mother street clothes to wear home. But Mama had balked when the gentleman in a blue hospital volunteer jacket came to take her downstairs in a wheelchair.

"It is a hospital rule, ma'am," the volunteer said. "We don't want to risk you hurting yourself."

"Stuff and nonsense. I'm perfectly capable of—"

Dr. McCandless walked into the room. "What's all the ruckus, Ingrid? I could hear you halfway down the hall."

Mama's cheeks colored. "Royce, they're treating me like I'm a baby. I'm ready to go home. I've work to do."

"You deserve to be pampered once in a while." He gestured for the volunteer to leave. "Now, if you will allow me, my dear." He took her upper arm and eased her into the chair, kneeling to adjust the foot rests.

Alisa did a double take. Almost no one called Mama by her Christian name. And she most certainly hadn't ever heard Mama call Dr. McCandless by his first name.

She eyed the doctor. Probably in his sixties, his silver hair and upright posture gave him a distinguished appearance. Dressed as he was in a blue blazer and slacks, he would have looked at home at a fancy country club. His bedside manner and reassuring voice had made Alisa feel safe as a child and, as a mother, confident of his skills.

But what was this new tone of affection between the doctor and her mother?

Safely seated in the wheelchair, Mama said, "Would you get the flowers, honey? They're still so beautiful." Four large bouquets were situated on every available level surface.

"Sure." Alisa tucked the bag of her mother's things under her arm, gave two bouquets to her mother to carry in her lap and wrapped her arms around the other two vases filled with flowers. Mama's friends had certainly been generous.

"Ready now, away you go in your carriage, my dear." The doctor pushed Mama out the door toward the elevator with Alisa following close behind.

As they waited for the elevator, Alisa asked, "Did you get any instructions from Dr. Johansen for your home care?"

"Oh, it's all in the bag you have." Mama waved her bandaged arm in Alisa's direction.

"You'll need to have your bandages changed daily," Dr. McCandless said. "If you have trouble doing that for her, Alisa, give me a call. I can drop by for a few moments."

"It's very nice of you to offer." Alisa was pretty sure she could manage, but she sensed something else was going on here. Did the good doctor want an excuse to visit her mother? Amazed and generally pleased, Alisa thought that was likely the case. Her mother had worked hard all of her life. Papa had been gone for ten years. Having a gentleman friend would be good for Mama's morale.

In the elevator, the doctor said, "As her hands heal, Ingrid will need physical therapy, probably three times a week to start."

Mentally, Alisa groaned. The closest physical therapy facility was in Kalispell, thirty-five miles away. Up and back, plus the time spent in therapy, meant nearly three hours out of her workday. She'd have to make some adjustments in her schedule.

"When the time comes, Ingrid, I'd be happy to arrange my schedule to drive you to your appointments."

Alisa's brows shot up. Dr. McCandless had always had a busy practice. Little kids with runny noses and nasty coughs and their anxious mothers filled his office waiting room. How in the world was he planning to reschedule his patients?

Looking up at the doctor, Mama gave him a beatific smile. "That would be very sweet of you, Royce."

The elevator stopped, and Alisa's stomach did a flip. Had her mother's medication included a brain-altering ingredient? Alisa had never seen Mama act this way with any man.

Except her father.

* * *

After all the fuss and paperwork of getting Mama released from the hospital, and the surprising revelation about Mama and Dr. McCandless, it was almost noon before Alisa got her to the diner.

The entire kitchen staff stopped work to cheer and applaud when Mama walked in the kitchen door. A moment later, the waitstaff on duty popped in to do the same.

Obviously both pleased and embarrassed, Mama waved them off. "Go on with you. We've got customers to feed. No need to get stirred up over me. I'm fine."

Everyone went back to work except Nick. "We're all glad to have you back, Mama."

She lifted her chin. "So. You're a big deal chef, are you?"

"I know my way around a kitchen," he acknowledged.

She sniffed as though unimpressed. "And you didn't think to mention that? You'd rather get your hands dirty painting and fixing broken steps?"

A smile kicking up the corners of his lips, Nick shrugged. "Seems to me that's what you needed done."

"Humph. Now you're gonna learn my secret recipe and pass it on to somebody else?"

"I won't tell a soul." He made a zipping gesture across his lips, his twinkling eyes revealing his delight.

Alisa put her arm around her mother's shoulders. "Mama, I think you should go upstairs and rest for a while before you try to work. If we have to scratch the special tonight—"

"Nonsense. I've been doing nothing but sleep for three days. Bring me a stool. I want to watch this young man make my dumplings. They gotta be just right. Our customers will know."

Nick quickly retrieved a stool from across the room and set it right beside his workstation, then helped her up onto it.

"Okay, Mama. Fire away. Teach me what I need to learn."

Alisa stood nearby watching the two of them at work, teacher and student. He was so eager, it was obvious why he'd been sent to Le Cordon Bleu for training. And why he'd succeeded as a chef.

Mama had taught Alisa her technique to make Czech dumplings years ago, but she hadn't really had the touch to get them to come out quite right. Nick was devouring the lesson. She was happier out front with the customers rather than being stuck in the kitchen where it was often twenty degrees hotter than in the restaurant area. Nick belonged here preparing food in the same way an artist worked with his paint and brushes. This was Nick's medium.

A pity he was only filling in until Mama could get back to work.

Feeling like a third wheel, Alisa wandered out to the front, her realm, unlike Mama's and Nick's in the kitchen.

Things were quiet. Automatically, she picked up a damp cloth and started to wipe the menus clean of sticky fingerprints and spilled syrup.

Jolene strolled over between serving customers. "I saw you brought Mama home. How is she feeling?"

"Stubborn. She won't go upstairs to take a rest. Instead she's teaching Nick how to prepare her chicken and dumplings."

Jolene jerked back. "You're pulling my leg. I never thought she'd let anyone outside the family learn the secret of her dumplings."

"That's what she's doing. She did make him promise to never reveal her recipe to anyone else. He's a lot more than a short-order cook. He's a chef. Turns out Nick trained at Le Cordon Bleu in Paris."

"Well, isn't that something special." A smug smile curved her lips. "Not only is the guy cool in a crisis, good-looking, likeable as all get-out, but he cooks, too. Honey, I hope you're taking a real close look at him. He sounds like just what the doctor ordered."

"Ordered for what?" Alisa frowned. It sounded

like Jolene had elected herself the president of Nick's private fan club, extolling his virtues to anyone who'd listen.

Jolene laughed. "Honey, if you can't figure that out, you're hopeless." Still chuckling, she picked up the coffeepot and headed for the table of four.

Alisa watched her refill their mugs. *She* certainly hadn't ordered up a man like Nick, virtues or not. The very idea that she and Nick might someday…

She couldn't bring herself to finish the thought. She'd given up fanciful dreams years ago.

## *Chapter Ten*

"I don't know about you, Mama," Nick said. "But I'm bushed. Why don't we take a break? I think I've got a pretty good handle on the dumplings."

Mama looked both surprised and relieved by his suggestion. She'd been showing signs of fatigue the past half hour or so. No wonder, since they'd been making dumplings for three hours straight. Pain from her burns had begun to deepen the age lines in her face.

"Are you sure, young man? I can keep going if you need to."

He helped her off the stool. "You've got me beat, Mama. I'm going to get some air. You want me to help you upstairs?"

Alisa came into the kitchen through the swinging door to the front. "Mama? Are you all right?" The hint of concern laced her words.

"I'm fine, but Nick says he's tired. He's taking a break."

Nick handed Mama off to Alisa. "Your mother is one strong lady. Just like you," he said under his breath. "It might be time for a pain pill and a nap."

Alisa nodded and mouthed, "thank you." She led Mama up the stairs.

Exhaling, Nick went over to the sandwich station. Truth be told, he was tired. His leg ached, and he was hungry. He put together a turkey, cheese and tomato sandwich on rye, grabbed himself a pint of milk and took his lunch outside.

Rags whined when he spotted Nick.

"Yeah, I know. You want to go running." He released the dog, who shook his body from one end to the other. "Okay, boy, go find us a stick. Go on, fetch."

Rags raced off, and Nick sat down on the porch steps. Dark clouds were forming to the west, promising rain. That was a good thing. The ground was bone dry. A high fire danger warning had been issued for the surrounding forest.

He'd only taken a couple of bites of his sandwich when Rags returned carrying a dead pine branch about six feet long in his mouth.

"I don't know, buddy. That looks pretty ambitious to me." Setting his sandwich aside, he stood and broke two feet off the tip of the branch.

Rags eyed the larger, discarded section with evident longing.

"It's okay. We'll save that for another time." He held up the shorter piece, let Rags sniff it, then heaved the stick halfway to the motel.

Rags bounded after it.

Nick had settled down for a few more bites of sandwich when Alisa stepped out onto the porch. He glanced up and smiled. She looked almost as tired as her mother had. The stress of keeping the diner going on her own was beginning to show. "Mama okay?"

"I got her to take a pain pill. She's resting on the couch. I'm pretty sure she'll fall asleep." She looked out toward the approaching clouds. "Thank you for pretending it was you who needed a rest."

"I was hungry, too. Figured we both needed a break."

Racing back with his stick, Rags leaped up the steps past Nick and proudly presented it to Alisa.

A youthful giggle escaped as she picked up the stick. "Your dog is fickle. He should've given you the stick."

"Not fickle. He's trying to make points with the pretty lady who brings him yummy scraps."

She failed to squelch her smile. "Just like a guy, huh? Always an agenda." She gave Rags a good pat and scratched him around his ears.

Nick wondered what agenda she thought he had.

Some guy had sure made her leery of men. Shame, too, because she was the kind of woman a man could get used to having around. If he was the right guy. And she'd let him. A privilege she appeared unwilling to grant him. Smart lady.

"Okay, fella, go get it." She threw the stick toward the back of the diner.

Just then Greg appeared. He spotted Rags and raced him to the stick. Rags won but was overwhelmed with joy to see the boy. They trotted back to the porch together.

Alisa went down the steps to meet him. "Hey, munchkin. You have a good day at school?" She gave him a hug, which he shrugged off. His lips were turned down in an almost cartoonish sad face that broadcasted it had been a lousy day at school.

"Mom, they're having a father-son fishing contest on Saturday. Pete and his dad are entering. So's Shaun and his dad. I was thinking maybe..." He turned to Nick, who got a sick feeling in the pit of his stomach. He knew what it was like to not have a father, not one that took him fishing or hunting or even bowling. But he wasn't qualified to be anyone's dad. And he didn't dare get close to Greg because he'd be leaving soon.

"Sorry, sport. I wouldn't be much help in a fishing contest. I've never caught a fish in my life." The tangled line with a hook that he'd once dropped into the lake hadn't fooled a single fish, assuming there had been any around.

The boy's hopeful expression crumbled. Alisa's pained look mimicked her son's disappointment.

"I could go fishing with you, munchkin," she volunteered.

"You're a mom. Not a dad," Greg grumbled.

"Okay. Then we'll think of something else fun to do on Saturday," Alisa promised, the shine of tears in her eyes.

His lower lip sticking out, Greg shoved his hands in the pockets of his jeans. A tear in the knee had ripped in what looked like a new pair.

"I never get to go fishin' like other guys." Head bent, shoulders hunched, he started up the steps.

"Wait! I have an idea," Alisa said.

Greg stopped and eyed his mother beneath lowered lashes. Nick figured an idea to go bowling wouldn't cut it with Greg. Not for this Saturday.

"Fishing can't be that hard," she said. "Papa's old boat is in the shed. There's a motor, although I can't guarantee it runs after all this time. And up in the rafters there's fishing gear. Rods and reels. Maybe some lures, I don't know." Her father had rarely taken time off to go fishing, and she could only remember going with him once or twice. "But if Nick could put it all together—"

Nick rocketed to his feet. "Now wait a minute.

Even if I could get the motor running and get some line tied onto a reel, we'd never catch anything. I don't even know how to cast. Or what lure to use."

"We could learn together," Greg said in a heart wrenching, pleading voice that was impossible to ignore or refuse.

Grimacing, Nick squeezed his eyes closed. He hadn't expected to get this close to the boy. Or care so much. "I don't know, kid. You know we'd probably lose."

Greg lifted his chin. "Mom always says it's not about winning. It's about showing up and playing the game."

*Wise mother!* Alisa had her lower lip pulled between her teeth waiting for Nick's decision, her son's plea reflected in the shine in her eyes.

"I shouldn't have suggested...you don't have to," she said.

Yeah, he did have to. He might not be the boy's father but he could act like it for a day. Fill in for the real deal like he was filling in for Mama as the diner's chief cook. Every kid should have a chance to go fishing. Nick was long overdue himself.

"Looks like you've got a fishing partner, sport. Let's go take a look at Papa's boat before I have to get back to work."

For a moment, the grateful smile on Alisa's face

made Nick feel like he could conquer anything, including the biggest lake trout around.

Guilt and relief battled in Alisa's chest as she went back inside. Guilt because Greg didn't have a father. That she'd foolishly picked the wrong man to love. Now her son was paying a price.

Relief, and renewed trepidation, churned through her because Nick had agreed to take her son fishing. That would be one more knot binding Greg to a man who would likely leave them. One more rung in a ladder of hero worship that went both up and down. And when it came down, it landed with a crash.

And she'd just orchestrated the same potential fall for *herself!*

Blowing out a sigh, she blamed the city fathers for organizing a father-son fishing event. Didn't they know some kids didn't have fathers? They could just as easily had a parent-child or grown-up friend-child event. Then none of the kids would have felt left out.

This year her son would be a part of the fun. But what about next year? Where would Nick be then?

Nick didn't work the Friday morning shift. Billy Newton, the regular morning short-order cook, handled the breakfast crowd. Instead, Nick headed directly to the maintenance shed. The chances of the outboard motor and ancient fishing gear working like they should seemed slim.

The storm that had come in during the evening, keeping the diner crowd light, had blown past, leaving only a few puffy clouds lingering behind in a pale blue sky.

It took just a few tries at starting the motor to confirm Nick's fears. Whatever gas had been left in the twelve-horsepower engine had turned to varnish.

The fishing poles looked all right, but the lines on the reels were permanently coiled. No one would be able to cast the line more than a few feet from the boat.

He didn't have a clue which of the lures he found in a tackle box would tempt a fish.

He stuffed everything except the boat itself into the back of his truck.

"Come on, Rags. Let's see if we can find someone to help us out." He hated the thought of letting Greg down. He remembered what that kind of disappointment felt like—a knife right square in the middle of his chest.

From his drive around the area on Sunday, he remembered an auto repair garage on the outskirts of town. He found it easily enough and parked next to a couple of dusty cars that looked like junkers.

Inside, a couple of cars were up on hoists and a

pickup sat waiting for attention. No one seemed to be around.

He strolled toward the back of the building where a big door was raised, revealing a swing set and a house built of logs. Nice digs, he thought, as Rags went to explore the area.

“May I help you?”

He turned at the sound of a female voice. An attractive woman with long, brown hair stood in the doorway of a glass-enclosed office.

“I was looking for a mechanic. I’ve got an outboard motor that’s stuck solid. I figured a mechanic would know how to fix it.”

“I’m sure he does. My husband just went to get something in the house. He’ll be right back.”

“Great. I’ll wait.”

Nick did a double take as Rags came trotting back into the garage. Puzzled, he knelt. “What have you got, boy?”

“Kitty Kat!” The woman raced across the garage. “Oh my! Is she hurt? She belongs to my daughter.”

“Give, boy. Give.” Gently, Nick took the young cat from Rags’ mouth. He stood, petting the calico with black, white an orange markings. She seemed to be no worse for wear.

“Is she all right?” the woman asked.

“Looks like it.” He handed her the cat.

“Shame on you for sneaking out of the house,”

she crooned while checking the cat for injuries. "Your dog must have a very soft mouth. A hunting dog?"

"Not since I've had him." It hadn't occurred to Nick that Rags could be a trained hunting dog, possibly for pheasants or ducks. Or maybe he was so gentle at heart, he knew not to hurt other animals.

A guy in blue mechanic's overalls came out of the house. He had the physique of a man who worked hard and the walk of someone comfortable with himself.

"Adam, honey, this man needs some repairs on an outboard motor. And you must have let Kitty Kat out when you went inside."

"I did? I didn't even see her."

"Well, you take care of this gentleman, and I'll put her back where she belongs." She headed for the house.

"Your wife?" Nick asked.

"Yep. Janelle and I have been married for two whole weeks. She's my bookkeeper and business manager, too." The grinning mechanic extended his hand. "Adam Hunter. What can I do for you?"

Nick introduced himself and told him about the motor. He signaled Rags to heel as they strolled out to his truck. "You're a lucky guy, married to an attractive woman who's smart, too."

"Don't I know it. We've got two of the prettiest little girls you'll ever see."

Two daughters and only married two weeks? Nick wondered how that had worked out.

Adam hefted the motor and carried it to a workbench to examine.

Nick felt a punch of envy for Adam and his family, and quickly suppressed the feeling. "I'm supposed to take Alisa Machak's son fishing tomorrow," Nick said. "Is there any chance you could fix it today?"

"Alisa at the diner?"

"That's the one. I've been helping her out lately. In fact, the motor belonged to her father."

"No fooling? I heard Mama got hurt."

Nick gave Adam an update, then got back to the point. "About the motor?"

"Yeah, it's an old one. Not even an electric starter. I'm going to have to take it all apart and boil out all the goo that's inside." He thought for a moment. "For Alisa's kid, I'll get it done. Can you come back around four or five?"

"I'll be here."

Thanking Adam, Nick climbed back into his truck, and Rags hopped into the seat behind him. He'd seen some fishing gear at the barbershop. Maybe Ned could help him out with the rest of his problem.

He angle parked a couple of doors down from the barbershop. Grabbing the ancient rods and reels, he strolled into Ned's shop.

"Hey, Nick. If you're planning to go fishing, you've missed the lake by about a hundred yards." Standing beside the barber chair, Ned was working on a gray-haired fellow with a mustache.

"I thought I'd just hook up with that fish on the wall in your back room. Figured that'd be easier than catching one myself."

Ned barked a laugh. "Not gonna happen, buddy. That prize was hard-won."

Parking himself in a chair, Nick propped the rods against the wall. Rags sat on the floor next to him, keeping his eye on Ned.

"I've got a fishing problem," Nick said. "Thought maybe you'd be a good one to help me."

"Sure. I'll be done with Jessup here soon." Using an electric razor, he buzzed the back of the man's neck.

As promised, it didn't take Ned long to finish the haircut and send his customer out the door.

One look at the old poles and Ned shook his head. "You're not going to catch much with these."

Nick told him about Greg and the father-son fishing contest. And his lack of experience fishing for anything.

Ned hooked his arm over Nick's shoulders. "You have lived a sadly deprived life, my friend."

The next thing Nick knew, he was out in the alley behind the barbershop learning to cast a lure on Ned's gear. After a half hour of practice, he knew he wasn't going to be great at this fishing business, but with a prayer and the Lord's help, maybe he and Greg wouldn't look like total fools out on the lake.

Maybe, if the fishing contest went okay, Alisa would even give him a smile and forget for a minute that he was an ex-con.

Midmorning, Alisa was carrying two orders of waffles and bacon to a couple sitting at the counter when Dr. McCandless walked into the diner.

"Good morning, Doctor. Help yourself to a seat at the counter or a table. I'll be right with you."

"Actually, I didn't come for breakfast. I had a break in my appointments. I thought I'd drop by, see how Ingrid is doing."

"Oh. That's very nice of you." Alisa had never known the doctor to leave his office and patients in the middle of the day. "She had a restless night. About three o'clock this morning, I made her take a pain pill. She complains they make her head feel like it's full of cotton balls."

"That's probably true. Still, she needs to take them so she can rest properly. I'll go on up and change her bandages."

"Um, Doctor, I already did that this morning."

"Oh, well…I'll just take a look." He headed for the stairs.

Still holding the plates of waffles, Alisa stared

after him, her brows lifting with curiosity. Was he actually making a house call? Dr. McCandless, a pediatrician, certainly wasn't Mama's regular doctor.

Or was this a social call?

# *Chapter Eleven*

Nick was in the kitchen setting up for the dinner hour when Greg burst in from school.

Breathless, the boy gasped for air. "Did you get the motor fixed for the boat?"

"Sure did, sport. I borrowed some top-of-the-line fishing gear, too, and we're all set to go."

"All right!" Greg pumped his fist in the air. "I told Pete and Shaun and everybody we're gonna catch the biggest fish they ever saw."

"I don't know about that, son." The youngster's eagerness tickled Nick. And made him nervous. He'd learned as a kid that if you get your hopes set too high, more often than not you end up disappointed. "Remember I've never caught anything, so don't be surprised if we get skunked and somebody else wins."

"Don't worry. We're gonna be the best fishermen in all of Bear Lake. I can feel it right here." He thumbed his puffed up chest.

The tightness in Nick's chest was telling him something different. "We have to be at the municipal dock early to get registered and get our boat in the water."

The swinging door opened, and Alisa walked in. She was dressed for work but hadn't yet pulled her hair back into a ponytail. "Hey, munchkin. You're home from school."

Greg raced over to his mom. "Nick got the motor fixed! We're gonna catch tons of fish, Mom. I know we are."

Laughing, she gave him a hug. "I hope so, honey, but you never know when the fish are going to bite. Even if you don't catch any fish at all, you'll still have fun."

"But we will, Mom! I know we will!" He dropped his backpack on a nearby chair. "I'm gonna go call Pete and tell him we're gonna be there real early in the morning." He ran out, his feet soon thundering on the stairs up to the family's quarters.

Nick perched on the edge of a stool with his back to the reflections in the stainless steel dishwashing machine—a habit he'd developed to avoid the images that could still taunt him. "I hope he won't be too disappointed if we don't catch anything."

"I guess disappointment is part of growing up."

She glanced around the kitchen, her eyes alert for anything that might need her attention. Hector was busy at his station, the scent of hamburgers rising from the grill. The dishwasher was whooshing along doing its job. "What time did you plan to leave in the morning?"

"I'd like to leave about seven. I'll hook up the boat trailer to my truck tonight before I turn in."

"I'll have him ready to go then. In fact, I doubt he'll sleep at all tonight. He's always been like that on Christmas Eve, too excited to sleep." Her gentle smile spoke of happy memories.

After Nick's mother died there hadn't been any reason for him to be excited about Christmas. Just another day as far as his dad was concerned.

Pressing aside the thought, Nick pushed up from the stool. "Maybe I ought to run over to the grocery store, see if I can buy a couple of trout to hang on Greg's hook."

She opened her mouth in a gasp. "But that would be cheating."

He grinned.

"Oh, you!" Her cheeks colored and she laughed. "You were teasing, weren't you?"

"Desperate times call for desperate measures," he said with a straight face, and loving the sound of her laughter. "We don't want to disappoint the boy, right?"

"Somehow I don't think a couple of gutted fish from the market would make him feel any better."

They stood four feet apart looking at each other for a long minute. Nick couldn't help but think of how beautiful she was when she blushed. And how he'd like run his fingers through her hair. And kiss her again.

It hurt to realize that none of that was going to happen no matter how much he wanted it.

Alisa was the one who couldn't sleep. She tossed and turned half the night fretting about Greg. Did Nick have life jackets? She'd seen to it that Greg had learned to swim. But if he fell out of a boat with all of his clothes on, would he stay afloat? The lake was so cold, hyperthermia could set in in a matter of minutes.

Did Nick know how to swim? Would he be able to rescue Greg if her son fell in the water?

For that matter, what was she thinking, sending her precious boy fishing with a near stranger who had once hurt a man so badly that he'd been sent to prison?

If only she could go with them and watch over Greg herself.

When it was finally time to get up, her head was as fuzzy as Mama's was on pain meds. She made sure that Greg, despite his excitement, ate breakfast. When they went downstairs, Nick had already pulled his truck and boat trailer up next to the diner. He was leaning against the fender waiting, his legs crossed at the ankle. Rags's nose was pressed against the back window.

Greg strutted right to the truck to climb inside.

"Wait a minute, young man." Alisa snared Greg by the back of his jacket. "Don't I get a kiss?"

"Ah, Mom, we gotta go." He barely relented enough for her to give him a hug and a kiss.

"Now you be careful, honey. Don't rock the boat or goof off, okay?"

"Yes, Mom. Now can I go?"

She released her son, and when she looked up she found Nick grinning at her, the crease in his cheek clearly visible. An unexpected flutter of awareness caught her off guard. She must be more fuzzy-headed than she'd thought.

"He'll be fine, Alisa. I promise to take good care of him."

"I know that but..." Her breath caught, which didn't have anything to do with Nick's winning smile or the way his blue eyes crinkled at the corners, she told herself. "Do you have life jackets? There may be some in the shed."

"Ned loaned me life jackets for both of us. I've also made us a couple of sandwiches in case we get hungry and a thermos of hot chocolate. I've got bottled water and sunscreen, too."

"Oh." All she'd been worried about was Greg drowning. "You're taking the dog?"

"I didn't want to leave him here. He'll be fine in the boat."

A frown pulled her eyebrows down. How could he know that? Rags might panic and try to get out. He could upset the whole boat.

With two long strides, Nick reached her. He tipped her chin up. "You going to wish us good luck?"

She was excruciatingly aware of the touch of his fingers beneath her chin. She swallowed hard. "Yes, of course. Good luck." Her voice sounded hoarse to her own ears.

"Thanks." Leaning forward, he pressed a kiss to her forehead. "Try not to worry."

"Come on, Nick. We're gonna be late," Greg insisted.

Nick stepped back, held her gaze for an instant then turned to jog around the truck and hop in the driver's side.

A big grin on his face, Greg waved as the truck and boat trailer pulled away. The name *Dreamer* painted on the side of the aluminum boat gave Alisa a jolt. Her father had been such a dreamer. Once upon a time, so had she.

Rooted in place, Alisa watched the truck turn on to the main road through town. Only when it was out of sight did she exhale the breath she'd been holding. Even so, the warmth of Nick's lips lingered on her forehead.

Why did he have to kiss her?

And why, of all the crazy notions, did she wish he'd kissed her on the lips?

Trying to ignore her foolish thoughts, she went upstairs. Mama, still dressed in her nightgown and robe, was sitting at the kitchen table. Her arms and hands were covered with the white cream the doctor had given her.

She flexed the fingers of her right hand to keep them limber despite the burns. "Did the boys get off all right?"

Alisa sat down opposite her. "They're off all right. But I'd hardly call Nick a boy." Just the opposite, he was all man and all wrong for her.

Mama eyed her curiously. "Compared to my age, he's a boy."

Not to Alisa. "Is Dr. McCandless coming by this morning?"

"Are you changing the subject?"

"Of course not." Alisa made a careful study of the hangnail on her thumb.

"It is nice that Nick is taking your boy fishing, yes?"

"Greg's thrilled." Pushing back her chair, Alisa stood. "Which is all very well and good. But what about next year and the year after? Who will take Greg fishing then?" Her voice rose, and an ache caught in her throat.

"Maybe Nick will take him again."

"He's going to leave. You know he will." Tears burned in her eyes. Tears of regret. Tears of longing. Tears she was not going to shed.

"You don't know that, my *Alisova.*"

Mama's softly spoken words, her loving Czech nickname, made Alisa want to be held and rocked in her mother's arms again as she had been as a child. She wanted to be told everything would be all right. Her scraped knee would heal. Her broken heart would become whole.

Except she was a grown-up now. She knew words couldn't heal. And broken hearts could stay broken for a long time. Hers and her son's.

Pulling her hair back, she grabbed a clip to hold it in place. "I'm going to go see how the breakfast service is going."

The diner was her life. Her home. An attractive man drifting through town wasn't going to change that.

"There's something you need to do today," Mama said. "I haven't paid Nick for his work yet. He'd probably like cash, not a check. You can pay him this afternoon."

Cash. Not a check for a drifter. With a pocket

full of cash he could travel light. No baggage. No commitment.

For Nick, Alisa and her son represented both.

After the lunchtime crowd thinned, Alisa went into the kitchen to prepare her order for Monday's delivery from the wholesale distributor. She'd barely sat down when she heard a cheer and applause rise from the front of the diner.

Jolene pushed open the swinging door. "Nick and your boy are back from fishing. You'd better come see."

Her first thought, that Greg might be hurt, propelled Alisa from her chair. She hurried out front only to be stopped by a crowd of a half dozen people crowded around one of the booths.

She pushed her way through. Nick and Greg were at the table, Nick with his arms looped leisurely across the back of the booth. In the middle of the table, a plump, eighteen-inch rainbow trout lay on a pile of newspapers. A gold-and-white trophy, as tall as the fish was long, stood beside it.

"Mom! Look what Nick and me caught!"

The crowd parted for Alisa. "That's a huge fish, honey. How in the world—"

"It was easy." Greg's eyes glistened with excitement. His grin could not have been broader. "At first, we didn't quite know what we were doing. Nick pushed our boat down the ramp, but he didn't get in fast enough so he got his shoes and pants all wet."

Nick acknowledged the truth of Greg's statement with a self-effacing shrug.

"We kind'a drifted around while Nick tried to start the motor," Greg continued, keeping his audience's rapt attention. "Everybody else was way out in the middle of the lake before we even got going."

"I should have practiced starting the motor yesterday," Nick conceded.

"But that was okay," Greg said. "We finally got out onto the lake and Nick was teaching me to cast, except we got our lines all tangled together."

"Not a smart move on my part," Nick said.

Alisa eased into the booth next to Greg. Fish perfumed the air and Greg's clothes. Probably Nick's as well.

"So Nick got us untangled but his hat blew off. I reached for it and almost fell out of the boat."

Alisa's heart squeezed. She'd been afraid of that. Her fingers trembled as she brushed a lock of hair away from his forehead.

"Nick grabbed the back of my jacket and pulled me back into the boat," Greg hastily explained. "I didn't even get wet."

"Thank goodness!" Alisa said on a sigh and caught Nick's gaze.

"I promised I'd take good care of him." Nick looked so at ease, not at all concerned that her son could have drowned, she could have strangled him. Or kissed him because he'd been quick enough to save her boy.

"So anyway." Greg drew the crowd's attention back to his story. "We cast our lines some more but we weren't catching anything. I was sort of bummed, you know?"

"I'm sure you were," Alisa said. "But you'd been warned that you might not catch any fish."

"I know. But I really wanted to. I even said a prayer but I wasn't sure God would care that much about whether I caught anything or not."

"He cares about you all the time," Alisa assured him. "But maybe He didn't want to take sides in the fishing contest."

"Yeah, that's sort of what Nick said. But it was getting late and we had to go back to the dock. Neither of us had even had a bite. We were getting skunked." A frown wrinkled Greg's forehead.

She glanced toward Nick, who had a smug grin on his face.

Greg drew a deep breath and continued. "Nick got the motor going again. I left my line in the water while he put-putted us back to shore. Then, all of a sudden, I got a huge yank on my line. I almost dropped my pole." The pitch of his young voice rose a notch and the words tumbled out of his mouth. "It practically bent my pole all the way down to the water."

"I thought he'd caught a rock on the bottom," Nick said.

"Yeah, but it wasn't a rock. It was a fish! I caught my very first ever fish, Mom. Isn't it the best-looking fish you ever saw?"

The crowd around them clapped and cheered. Alisa hugged Greg and kissed him on the top of his sweaty head.

Jolene slipped away to deliver her orders. Cassidy, a teenager who worked part-time at the grocery store as a stock boy, reached across the table to give Greg a congratulatory fist bump.

"As soon as we got back to shore," Nick said, "we took the fish to the judges to be weighed."

"We got second place, Mom. Can you believe that? I got a trophy and everything."

"I'm very proud of you, munchkin. Very proud."

"All Shaun and his dad caught were two fish about this big." Greg held up his hands about six inches apart. "And Pete didn't catch anything at all."

"That's too bad." Alisa was sure Greg's friends would be as disappointed about not catching any fish as Greg would have been. "Maybe they'll do better next year."

"No, Nick and me are gonna win first place next year. You just wait and see."

Nick gripped the back of Greg's neck in a

friendly vise. "I can't make that kind of a promise, sport. You know that."

Alisa's heart dropped to her stomach. Was Nick saying he'd be gone by next year's contest? Of course he was. He'd hadn't planned to stay in Bear Lake as long as he had.

Not bothered by Nick's unwillingness to make that promise, Greg eagerly told the rest of his fish tale.

"After we got our trophy and stuff, Nick said we had to clean the fish. That was all icky and gross and smelly, but Nick said if I was going to be a good fisherman, I had to do it."

Finally, he relaxed against the back of the pink, vinyl-covered booth, all dreamy-eyed. "Mom, this was the greatest day I've ever had!"

Dread of the future, the day she'd have to tell Greg that Nick was gone, roiled through her stomach. How was it possible that Nick wouldn't know the pain his leaving would cause her little boy? Maybe he'd never stuck around long enough to witness the damage he had done.

How could he care so little about those he left behind?

Later, as Nick was closing down the kitchen after a busy Saturday night, Alisa appeared.

"Mama asked me to pay you for your time so far." She handed him an envelope. "She thought you'd rather have cash than a check. Hope that's all right."

"Sure. Cash is fine." He opened the envelope and flipped through the twenty-dollar bills. Enough gas money to go a long way.

"Okay, then, I'll see you in the morning." Her posture rigid, she left the kitchen.

Nick heard her footsteps on the stairs and the creak of the floor above him when she reached the family quarters.

Idly, he weighed the envelope in his hand. He got a small disability pension from the army because of his leg. That went automatically into a bank account in Baton Rouge. When he needed money for food or gas, he'd stop at the first bank he came to and get them to arrange a transfer of funds. He didn't need much.

With the cash Alisa had given him, he could open a bank account here in Bear Lake. Close down the Baton Rouge account and have the disability check directed here. If he were going stay that would make sense.

He'd stuck around for more than a week. That was a long time based on his recent history.

But not long enough to quit running. Not yet.

That night when Nick went to bed, he figured he'd sleep like a rock. He'd had a great day and gotten lots of fresh air. That fish Greg had caught still made him chuckle. Lucky kid!

Rags on the floor beside the bed could barely keep one eye open. He'd had a big day, too.

Rolling to his side, Nick felt himself drifting off to sleep.

The dream started. Bullets ricocheting around the kitchen at the outpost. Explosions. Guys screaming. Panic twisting in Nick's gut.

And then the dream changed. The bullets were still there. Bombs exploding. Blood spraying all over the stainless steel prep tables. Except now he was running. Running after Alisa and Greg. He had to get them to safety. Get them away from the bullets that could rip at their flesh. Keep them from dying.

His legs wouldn't move. Sweat drenched his body. He couldn't get to them in time.

"Stop!" he shouted. "Not that way! Come with me."

Two armed insurgents blocked their way. They raised their rifles. Pointed them at Alisa and Greg.

Alisa screamed.

"Nooo!" Nick bolted upright, his own scream echoing in his head.

Rags's wet tongue swiped at the sweat on Nick's face. He drew a deep breath that burned in his chest. His heart hammered like the rat-a-tat of a machine gun. His head felt like it would explode.

*Dear God in heaven, please don't let anything happen to Alisa and Greg.*

Still locked in the aftermath of the dream, fear, as sharp as a fish-gutting knife, sliced through him. What if the only way he could protect Alisa and her son was to leave them?

# *Chapter Twelve*

Alisa held the umbrella over Mama as they walked into church on Sunday morning. Unperturbed by a little rain, Greg ran off toward his Sunday school class. The weather report called for scattered showers during the early hours with heavier rain later.

Alisa knew that the locals would likely skip brunch at the diner if the rain became a factor. The day's income for the diner would drop off appreciably.

She and her mother reached the open double doors and Dr. McCandless stepped out to greet them.

"Good morning, Ingrid. Alisa." Dressed in a dark suit and tie, he nodded formally to each of them in turn. "It's good to see you out and about, my dear." He extended his arm, and Mama took it.

They walked inside arm in arm, leaving Alisa startled and openmouthed, folding up her umbrella. When had her mother's relationship with the doctor become so strong with references to *my dear*. She vaguely remembered a couple times when Mama would leave the kitchen to visit with the doctor while he ate his early morning breakfast. But that had only happened occasionally, hadn't it? And maybe a dinner or two. She really hadn't paid that much attention.

Obviously, she'd been missing something.

Nick walked up beside her. "Is there anything wrong?"

She blinked, trying to bring her thoughts back to the present. Rain darkened the shoulders of Nick's omnipresent khaki jacket. If he was planning to stay in Bear Lake, he'd need to buy a warmer jacket soon. *If* being the operative word.

"No, nothing's wrong." She finished collapsing the umbrella and walked inside. She took a program from the greeter at the door. Behind her, she sensed Nick following her. His presence taunted her like a merry-go-round ring she couldn't quite grasp and shouldn't even try to reach. *If only* rarely came true.

Mama and Dr. McCandless had left room for her in their pew. She slid over beside the doctor.

Mama turned her head, spotted Nick in the aisle and waved to him. "There's room for you, too."

Rolling her eyes, Alisa wished her mother would

stick to her own business. This was no time for her to be playing matchmaker.

To halt an inexplicable urge to reach for his hand, she stiffened her shoulders and primly folded her hands in her lap when Nick sat down beside her. He brought with him the fresh scent of rain and the outdoors as well as the elemental masculine fragrance that was his own.

"Would you rather I sit somewhere else?" he asked under his breath. A frown pulled his dark brows together.

"Everyone is welcome in God's house." Biting her lip, she chided herself for being so snippy simply because Nick might soon leave town. That was hardly the Christian attitude she should convey in church. She forced her shoulders to relax and glanced at Nick. "Greg slept with his trophy last night."

His lips hitched into a smile. "If I'd won something like that as a kid, I would have too."

"I told him he shouldn't take it to school for show-and-tell tomorrow. I thought it might make the other boys envious."

"Good point. They'd probably snatch the trophy at recess and play keep-away with it."

Pleased that he'd agreed with her decision, Alisa turned toward the front of the church. The organ music rose. The congregation stood for the first hymn as Pastor Walker walked out in front of the choir, lifting his arms in welcome.

The rain had stopped, although the sky was still a threatening gray when the service was over. Alisa hoped it would stay that way for a few hours.

Greg came running toward her through the crowd of parishioners chatting with friends. Instead of coming to Alisa, he stopped in front of Nick.

"Hey, Nick. Did you bring Rags with you?"

"Yep. With the rain, I had to leave him in the truck."

"Can I let him out and take him for a walk?"

Nick dug in his jeans for the keys. "If it's okay with your mom. His leash is in the front seat." He tossed the keys to Greg, who dashed off without waiting for Alisa's approval.

She grimaced. "You're very trusting. I hope he doesn't drive off with your truck."

Frowning, he slid her a glance. "Hmm, I didn't think about that."

"When he's a few years older, you'd probably give that a second thought." She snapped her mouth shut. For a moment, she'd forgotten that in a few years, or maybe a few weeks, Nick wouldn't be anywhere near Greg or Bear Lake.

"Alisa, dear," her mother said. "You and Greg

can go on. I'm going to stay here with Royce. He'll bring me home."

Shooting Dr. McCandless a surprised look, Alisa said, "Sure. Okay."

"You see," the doctor said, "she and I are going on a little trip with the senior citizens group."

"A trip?" Alisa gaped at him.

"It's just twelve days," Mama assured her. "Since I won't be able to go back to cooking right away, Royce thought it would be nice to visit Yellowstone, Zion and Bryce Canyon and then go onto California. Your father and I never had a chance to see them when he was alive. This seems like a perfect time." She looked up at the doctor and smiled. "When I told Royce I'd always wanted to go there, he suggested we join the church bus tour."

"High time we both take a vacation," McCandless said with a youthful grin that belied his sixty-plus years.

"Mother, you can't go off with—" Alisa nearly choked. "I mean, it wouldn't be proper." What in the world was her mother thinking? For that matter, what would others think when they heard about the trip?

"Now don't you worry, *Alisova.* We'll be just fine." She patted Alisa's arm with her still injured hand. "There's nothing wrong with two friends going on a vacation together. I'll be sharing a room with Abigail Mayors, and we'll have all our friends from church to visit with."

That was a relief! But her mother— "What about the diner?"

"I'm sure you and Nick will be able to take care of any problems that might come up." She glanced at Nick. "Isn't that right?"

He shrugged. "Sure. We'll be fine. Don't worry about a thing."

"Jake called me yesterday," Mama continued. "His daughter is much better now and will be able to take care of herself. He'll be here by Tuesday at the latest, ready to get back to work."

Alisa whipped her head to Nick. She wanted to gain his support to keep Mama at home, only she found Nick appeared unconcerned about Mama's plans. He stood there, the tips of his fingers in his hip pockets, rocking slightly back and forth on his feet, a half smile on his face. She wanted to poke him in his chest. Didn't he realize that her mother was going away with a man? A man who wasn't her husband? Even it was a church sponsored trip—

Mama never would have condoned Alisa doing that; she was very much old country. Nor would Alisa have suggested it.

McCandless took Mama's arm. "I'll have your mother back home by dinnertime. The bus leaves in the morning, so she'll have to pack tonight." With that, the two of them strolled back into the church.

Alisa planted her fist on her hip. Why were they leaving so soon? Couldn't Mama have given her a chance to adjust to the whole idea of Mama and *Royce* going off together?

Looking around the almost empty parking lot, Nick said, "Bet they'll have a great time. That's really pretty country, particularly in the fall."

He would say that, she thought with annoyance.

"I'm going to go check on Greg and my dog," he said. "You coming?"

Oh, yes, she was coming. She trudged after him. Nothing like having her world tipped upside down in the course of only a few minutes. Especially when it meant she and Nick would be working closely together for twelve days.

Unless he bailed out on her like Ben had, leaving her on her own.

Late Wednesday night, after he'd spent some time with the vets at the barbershop, Nick chinned himself on the bar between the trees. He kept a mental count—twenty, twenty-one, twenty-two...

It had been three days since he and Alisa had waved goodbye to Mama and the doctor. They'd driven off in the doctor's SUV with four-wheel drive, both of them looking excited and glad to be on their way to the church and the waiting bus.

Alisa, on the other hand, had been in a stressed-out, blue funk ever since they'd left. Nick didn't understand that. Mama had a right to some happiness.

So did Alisa.

…forty. His muscles burning, Nick dropped to the ground to do his push-ups. Breathing hard, letting his heart rate slow, he looked toward the diner. It was late, the diner closed for the night, but there was still a light on in the kitchen. Nick had skipped out early to go to the vet's group at the barbershop. Had Hector forgotten to turn the lights off?

Or was Alisa still working?

Standing, Nick brushed his palms off on his jeans and strolled toward the kitchen door. Rags trotted along beside him. He'd check to make sure everything was all right and switch off the lights. Then he'd finish his workout.

The air felt chill and damp from a recent rain, and the sky was dark with clouds. Few cars passed on the highway, making the night eerily quiet.

He stepped up onto the porch and tried to doorknob. The door opened easily.

"Stay," he ordered Rags in a low voice.

Residual heat from the grill and ovens made the kitchen far warmer than the outside air. He eased past the prep stations, all cleaned and ready for the morning shift. In the dim light, reflections were indistinct and blurred. No one was in sight. The place felt deserted.

And then he heard a sob. Alisa!

He hurried to the back where there was a makeshift office and desk where Mama and Alisa did their paperwork, ordering supplies and paying bills.

Alisa had her head down on the desk that was covered with ledger sheets. Another sob shook her shoulders.

Nick hunkered down beside her and placed his hand on her back. His feelings for her lodged like a stone in his chest. "What's wrong, Alisa?"

She started, lifting her head. "Oh, Nick..." She reached for him, awkwardly wrapping her arms around his neck, and he held her while she sobbed, her head on his shoulder.

"Sh, sh," he repeated, stroking her back, wondering what could have set her off. Something about Greg? The kid had seemed fine when Nick saw him after school. Had Mama been hurt? With the roads slick with rain, there could have been a bus accident.

"Can you tell me what's wrong?" he pleaded. "Is it Greg? Your mother?"

Alisa lifted her head. She swiped her tears away with the back of her hand, which didn't do a thing for her red eyes or runny nose. Nick grabbed for a box of tissue on the desk and handed her one.

"I'm sorry. I'm not usually like this. But with Mama gone… I know it's only been three days." Straightening in her chair, she blew her nose. "It's not Mama. Or Greg. It's the business, the diner and motel."

Not sure what she meant, Nick dragged a nearby chair over to the desk and sat down. "What about the diner?"

"Since Mama's not here, I've been going over the accounts." She gestured toward the records spread out in front of her. "We've been losing money every month this year. Summer should have made up for any early losses, but it didn't. The price of food and supplies have gone up ten-percent or more since January. Today I got the bill for fire and liability insurance. It's nearly doubled!"

"Ouch. Did you have some claims against you last year?" Insurance companies could do that, jack up your rates if they had to pay out a claim. Or they could increase their rates on a whim.

"No, not a thing. To pay this, I'll have to take money out of our savings. But the fact is, we can't go on losing money every month and stay afloat. Mama hadn't said a word to me about losing money."

"She probably didn't want to worry you."

Exhaling, Alisa finger combed her hair back from her face. "Even if she'd told me, I don't know what I could do about it. I mean, we have to buy food for the diner, pay the staff. Handle the laundry for the motel and diner. We really need another waitress so I don't have to worry about both the front and the back. But there aren't that many places where we could reduce expenses and I don't see how we could find the extra to hire someone new."

"Tell you what, sweetheart." He took her hands and urged her to stand. Although the finances were the immediate problem, Nick suspected stress and overwork were at the crux of her tears. And maybe worry about Mama being away. "Not only did the army send me to Le Cordon Bleu, they had me take classes in how to manage a food service program." Those classes were pretty boring, but he'd dreamed of someday owning his own restaurant so he'd paid attention. "You're tired now and stressed out because your mother's not here."

Slipping his arm around her shoulders, he eased her through the kitchen toward the stairs.

"When there's a lull in the action tomorrow," he said, "you and I can sit down and go over the books. Take a good look at the menu, too. There may be places where you can save without downgrading your service."

She shook her head. "I don't know, Nick. I've tried to think of everything, but it doesn't add up to enough to cover the increased costs."

"Trust me on this. There's always a way. We just have to find it."

Nick left her at the bottom of the stairs, and Alisa climbed them by herself.

On the second floor, Alisa checked to see that Greg was okay. He'd thrown his covers off. She pulled them up so he wouldn't get chilled.

Her throat ached from the tears she'd shed. Her eyes felt like they'd been prodded by hot pokers. Her entire body had been drained of energy. She wanted nothing more than to curl up in Nick's arms.

Could he really know how to cut costs, figure out a way to make the diner profitable in the face of increasing costs? Or was he just saying that so she'd temporarily forget the truth?

A part of her desperately wanted to rely on Nick. To believe he'd have the answers.

She walked to the window, pulled back the curtain. The light was on in his room across the way.

Would it be foolhardy to trust a man again? To let her heart rule her head? To believe Nick when he called her sweetheart?

## *Chapter Thirteen*

After his morning run with Rags, Nick went to the diner to have breakfast.

He'd had a restless night, but not because of nightmares this time. Instead he'd been tossing and turning trying to figure out where to cut corners on the diner's budget without impacting the quality of service. For the first time, he wished he'd kept the notes the instructor had handed out in the class.

When he pushed open the diner's door, the tempting scents of bacon sizzling on the stove, freshly baked sweet rolls and brewed coffee greeted him. Inhaling deeply, he sat down at the counter.

Moments later, Jolene arrived with a steaming mug of coffee.

"Hey, Nick. How's it going?"

"Can't complain. How 'bout you?" He dragged the mug closer and wrapped his hands around it.

"I could complain, mostly about my adolescent children, but it wouldn't do any good." She chuckled. "What can I get you today?"

"Billy in the back sure is making the bacon smell real tempting this morning and the sweet rolls too. Plus a couple of eggs over easy will do."

"You got it."

"Where's Alisa this morning?"

"She went upstairs to check on Greg getting ready for school. Don't worry." Jolene winked at him. "She'll be back soon."

"Great." He frowned a little as Jolene went off to place his order. What had that wink been for? He had the distinct impression that Jolene thought he and Alisa had something going on between them. No matter how much he liked the idea, that wasn't going to happen.

He swiveled around to size up the customers. About three-quarters of the booths were occupied, mostly with families with young children plus some couples on their own. Tourists, he imagined. They rarely got an overflow crowd for breakfast so the banquet room was dark.

Taking a gulp of coffee, he wondered where area businesses held their meetings. Probably Sandy's Lakeside Restaurant, a more upscale restaurant than the diner. Still, there had to be a way to pick up some of that business.

He turned back to the counter just as Alisa arrived with his breakfast. Based on the dark circles under her eyes, she hadn't slept any better than he had.

"How are you feeling this morning?" he asked.

"A little gluey eyed," she admitted.

"If you're still worried about the diner running at a loss, don't be. There are lots of ways we can improve the bottom line."

"If you say so." She reached for the coffeepot and filled up his mug.

He grinned at her. "Trust me."

"Yeah, that's what all the guys say." Her lips tilted with the hint of a smile before she carried the coffeepot down the counter to fill another customer's mug.

About midmorning, Alisa sat down at the desk in the back of the kitchen. Nick pulled up a chair beside her.

"Okay, let's take a look at what you've got," he said.

She turned the ledger around so he could read it. "I suppose we could reduce the number of items on our menu, but that might shrink the number of customers we get."

"First we'll take a look at the top ten food items you spend the most on every month."

Her forehead tightened. "I'll have to get that from the invoices." He waited while she pulled the wholesaler's folder from the nearby filing cabinet. Aware that they were sitting very close together, close enough that she caught the pleasant scent of coffee on his breath, she scanned the most recent invoice. "Chicken quarters for the special are always a big item."

"Okay." He reached across the desk to grab a sheet of scratch paper and a pencil. He started a list. "Chicken quarters. What's next?"

His arm had brushed her hand as he had stretched to get the paper, leaving a band of residual warmth. "Hamburger meat."

"You buy that in bulk?"

"No, in ready-formed patties."

"There's a place where you could save. You'd lose some efficiency, but it could save you several cents per burger."

"A few cents won't help much."

"Won't it?" he challenged. "How many burgers do you serve a week?"

She eyed his jaw closely, noticing that he'd cut himself while shaving. The urge to kiss-it-and-make-it-all-better came out of nowhere. She quickly shoved the thought aside and did the calculation. "I see what you mean."

He put a check mark beside ground beef. "You can probably negotiate a better deal if you buy more and store the extra in your freezer. If you've got room."

Alisa considered that possibility and thought it might work. Continuing through the invoices, she named several other items that were at the top of the expense list. He came up with ways to reduce the cost, assuming the wholesaler would cooperate.

"You're good at this," she said.

"Despite what you've heard about the government, the army really does try to keep their expenses down and still feed the troops decent meals."

"You really liked being in the army, didn't you?"

"It was like belonging to a real family." He shuddered a bit, then glanced away, staring unfocused into the distance. "I hadn't had much of that when I was growing up."

Her heart aching for the boy he'd been, she touched his arm. "I'm sorry."

"Yeah, well..." He shrugged off the moment. "I'll call your wholesaler, see what kind of a deal I can make on these items you buy the most. Meanwhile, let's talk about how we can make better use of the banquet room."

That suggestion stopped her as well as his slip into talking about *we* instead of her. She suppressed her need to ask him about that. "We have a few birthday and anniversary parties in there. Plus it fills for Thursday night specials and on holidays like Easter and Mother's Day."

"Okay. But what you need to do is look for regular events. Business sales meetings. Social clubs that get together weekly or monthly."

"Most of those go to Sandy's Lakeside Restaurant."

"So let's talk to some of the groups about meeting here. I'd guess our prices are cheaper. Still good food. You know most everybody in town. Ask around."

She worried her lower lip. "Wouldn't that be unethical? Trying to steal customers from Sandy's? They're really good people. I don't want to turn them into enemies."

"Maybe you don't steal. You make up a banquet flyer with choices and the prices. If we're competitive with Sandy's, folks will come to us. It will be their decision."

Considering the possibility, she nodded. "That might work. I'll have to check with Mama."

"I understand. Now, let's talk about a take-out menu. Every time I drive by the Pee-Wee Drive-In, they're busy. We could attract customers who want a little more than just a burger and fries yet don't want to take time to eat a sit-down meal."

"I'd never thought of that."

Nick leaned back in his chair. "I was thinking last night about how popular the Thursday special is. How 'bout we add a Tuesday night special?"

"Oh, that would be too much for Mama to handle. You know it isn't easy to make those dumplings and terribly time consuming."

"I was thinking more along the lines of an all-you-can-eat spaghetti and salad special. That's a low-cost meal and high profit. Kids would love it."

She cocked her head. "Are you talking about using your mother's recipe for the sauce?"

"Authentic Italian pasta sauce. Sounds like a match for authentic Czech dishes, doesn't it? Can't do the homemade pasta though, not and keep the price low enough to appeal to families."

Her heart did an extra beat. Was Nick suggesting that he'd stay in Bear Creek? Make the spaghetti sauce himself?

"I, um… That sounds like a great idea."

His grin creased his cheek and made her heart take tumble.

The number of cost-cutting and increased sales ideas Nick tossed out astounded Alisa. He might be a trained chef, but at heart he was a solid businessman. The kind of businessman who would make an excellent partner. *If* he were planning to stay in Bear Lake.

Which, if it was a part of God's plan, might just be the case.

They made it through the weekend without Mama, and Alisa was feeling pretty good about implementing some of Nick's ideas for the diner.

On Tuesday, he negotiated a deal with their wholesale distributor that would save the Pine Tree Diner nearly a thousand dollars a month.

The man was a genius!

Hearing Greg's voice outside, she knew he was home from school and had engaged Rags in yet another game of fetch. Smiling, she stepped out onto the porch. Nick was sitting on the lower step watching the action.

"Looks like Rags has become my boy's best friend," she said.

Nick glanced up at her. "Or maybe it's the other way around."

She sat down on the step above his. "I've always told him he couldn't have a dog because we can't have animal hair all over the place in the diner. Maybe I should reconsider." Her son had never been happier than he had been since Rags and Nick had arrived in Bear Lake.

Despite her best efforts, she couldn't quite squelch the admission that she liked having Nick around too. And his dog.

Greg and Rags came running back toward the diner.

"Hey, Mom. Guess what?"

"The moon is made of green cheese," she teased.

Her son's jaw came unhinged. "Huh?"

"Come here, silly. Let me give you a hug."

Dutifully, Greg came close enough for a quick

hug before hopping off the steps. "I was gonna tell you that tomorrow is a teachers' institutional day."

"Institutional?" Nick echoed. "I remember a few teachers who needed to be—"

"Hush," she admonished him with a laugh. "Are you sure you don't mean institute day, honey?"

"Yeah, somethin' like that." Greg knelt in front of Rags and got a full-face lick of approval. "Anyway, there isn't any school tomorrow. I thought maybe we could all do something together."

All, meaning that Nick and Rags should be part of whatever they did.

"Greg, I don't know. With Mama still away—"

"I think that's a great idea. We could all use a day off. Hector and Billy Newton can handle cooking during the day, but I'll need to be back in time to prepare dinner." Standing, Nick leaned against the hand railing, lifting his brows as if to say she needed the break more than anyone else. "What'd you have in mind, sport?"

"We could go fishing." The twinkle in Greg's eyes, and the hope Alisa saw there, brought a lump to her throat.

"I don't know, sport. I borrowed all that gear from Ted, and that was for a special occasion. I don't want to bug him to borrow his stuff all the time."

Some of the excitement left Greg's eyes. "You could go buy some more fishing stuff just for us."

"Gregory Andrew Machak! We do not ask people to spend their hard-earned money on us. Do you understand?"

The boy hung his head and kicked at the dirt with the toe of his shoe.

Nick knelt down to Greg's level. "Tell you what, we don't have to fish to have a good time. The weather's supposed to be good tomorrow during the day. I bet your mom knows a good place to picnic on the other side of the lake. We could take the boat, spread out a blanket when we get there. Maybe toss a ball around and skip rocks in the lake. How does that sound?"

Greg eyed Alisa from under his long eyelashes.

She held her breath. It sounded like a great idea for Greg. Less so for her. Picnics were things families did together. The thought of storing up that kind of a memory for both her and her son frightened her. The memory might be too hard to forget.

"What do you think, Mom?" Nick asked with a teasing glint in his eyes that matched the hope in Greg's. "We could leave after the breakfast rush and be back in plenty of time to get ready for the dinner crowd."

Alisa blew out a sigh. They were double-teaming her. How could she possibly say no to such an innocent sounding outing when she knew how much her son wanted it?

"All right, you two. A picnic it is. I'll pack us some lunch in the morning."

Greg cheered. "Come on, Rags. We all get to go on a picnic tomorrow." The two of them went racing off.

She forced her lips into what she hoped resembled a smile. "How is it I feel like I was tricked into that?"

His grin brought out that special dimple in his cheek. "Because you've got a very persuasive son?"

Right. And when it came to Nick, she had the potential to be a very foolish woman.

She heard the phone ring in the kitchen. A moment later, Hector stuck his head out the door. "Your Mama's on the phone. She wants to talk to you."

"Great." She asked Nick to send Greg inside when he'd worn himself out, and hurried into the kitchen. There were so many things she wanted to say to her mother, and so many questions she wanted to ask. Although some of her deepest questions she wasn't yet ready to articulate.

She answered the phone at the desk in the back. "Hi, Mama, how's your trip going?"

"It's been wonderful, dear. I'd never imagined how spectacular the national parks are. We all wish the trip would never end. We're having a wonderful time."

*We?* Apparently she and Dr. McCandless were getting along just fine.

"How is it going at the diner?" Mama asked.

"We're managing all right, but we all miss you."

"And Nick? Is he still there?" Mama's question seemed hesitant.

She rubbed her hand along the back of her neck. "Not only here, but he's helping me with some ideas to cut our expenses." Briefly, she told her mother about some of Nick's ideas about cutting costs. "We can talk about that when you get home."

"My, my. It sounds like he's quite a smart businessman."

"That's some of the training he got in the army, running a restaurant." Alisa took a deep breath and swallowed. "He's also taking Greg and me on a picnic tomorrow. Greg has the day off from school."

"See, I told you he was a good man. He'd be a good father, too, Alisova."

Alisa knew it was way too soon to talk about that. "So when are you coming home, Mama?"

"We get home Friday. My hands are healing well. I'm ready to get back to work."

"That's wonderful, Mama. We'll all be glad to have you home again. But don't feel you have to rush getting back to work. Your doctor said it would take six weeks to heal."

"We'll see, dear, when I get home."

* * *

After Greg went inside for snack and homework, Nick tied up Rags and followed Greg into the diner to start dinner prep.

He cut up bacon, carrots, celery, potatoes and some fresh garlic, put the ingredients in a large saucepan over high heat to start the minestrone soup de jour. As he stirred the pot, he realized he wasn't squinting to ward off the nightmarish reflections in the stainless steel counters.

A definite step forward. Though he wasn't going to intentionally push his luck by staring at reflective surfaces.

Going on a picnic with Alisa and Greg was a good move, too. That made him feel almost normal. In general, his nightmares had been less intrusive, less frightening the past few nights. Maybe he could actually hang around Bear Lake longer than he had anticipated.

He smiled as he poured beef stock into the sizzling pan. The surprise in Alisa's eyes when he had jumped on the idea of a picnic had tickled him. She'd been so stressed with Mama gone, she needed a break even more than he did.

A picnic wasn't a lifetime commitment. He couldn't make that grand a promise. Not now. Maybe not ever. But he could promise a few hours.

It would be fun.

* * *

Feeling more lighthearted than she had in a long time, Alisa slid the ice chest into the back of Nick's truck. She'd keep her tote bag with her up front. *Imagine, a day off!* Well, most of a day at any rate.

The highest peaks on the mountains east of Bear Lake had received a dusting of snow from the last storm that had passed through. Now, the midmorning sun glistened off of that snow as if it were covered with diamonds.

Finished hooking up the boat trailer to the truck, Nick came up beside her. "You about ready to go?"

She glanced at her tote. "I think so."

"What's in there?"

"The usual—sunscreen, some snacks and a couple of bottles of water, a blanket to sit on, a magazine to read if I have a chance, a first aid kit if anyone gets hurt."

"Sounds like you're prepared to stay a week," he teased.

"With a nine-year-old boy, you never know what might happen in the next fifteen minutes."

"Yeah, I get that. I went out earlier to the general store and bought some life jackets. But I'm hopeful neither of you will fall overboard. That lake water is seriously cold. Bought a life jacket for Rags, too."

"I'm sure he'll look adorable."

"We'll see if he agrees." Turning toward the back of the motel, he let out a shrill, two-note whistle.

Alisa winced. "Are you calling Rags or Greg?"

"Chances are good they'll both come."

As he spoke, Rags rounded the corner at the back of the motel followed by Greg running full blast.

"He's really excited," she said. "It's very kind of you to let him talk you into doing this."

"He's a neat kid. And I could use a break, too."

Smiling at her son as he slid to the stop in front of Nick, Alisa realized just how much Greg wanted a father, a male role model in his life. A man to look up to. A man to teach him how to be a man.

Squeezing her eyes shut, she desperately tried not to wish for something neither she nor her son could have.

With the help of a bystander, Nick launched the boat at the municipal dock. With the ice chest already in the boat, Alisa climbed in with her tote to sit at the bow. Greg followed with Rags, both taking the middle seat. Nick took his place at the stern and the bystander shoved them off.

"Let's see if I can get this thing started this time." Nick pulled hard on the starter cord of the outboard motor. It sputtered once then turned over with a reassuring roar.

Greg cheered. "You did it, Nick!"

He laughed, as proud as if he'd just set foot on

the moon. "In one try!" After adjusting the throttle, he set them on a course across the lake.

"Where to, Ms. Machak?" he asked, shouting over the rumble of the motor.

She pointed toward a notch in the far hillside. "Arrowhead Cove. Very peaceful."

"You got it!" He turned slightly north.

"Can I steer?" Greg asked.

"Sure. Come sit back here with me."

The boat rocked as Greg changed positions. Alisa turned to look out over the bow. The wind blew in her face, brushing her hair back. Her cheeks felt the kiss of the sun, and she felt a sense of peace. A feeling that this was right, the place she was meant to be.

God could not have led a good man like Nick back to Bear Lake without a purpose. He may have served time in prison, but at his core he wasn't a criminal. She would sense that if it were true. Her heart would know.

Their boat raised a raft of mallards that had been floating comfortably on the gently undulating water. With much flapping of wings and noisy quacking, they took off only to land thirty feet away to resume their bobbing journey.

A conifer forest of fir, pine and larch covered the far hillside with an occasional splash of yellow to announce the presence of a stand of aspen trees. As she watched the shoreline, a bald eagle swept down to the water, snared a fish in its talons and lumbered up to a tree top with its heavy load.

"Did you see the bald eagle, Greg?" she called back to him. "He just caught a fish."

"Nuh-uh." His focus seemed entirely fixed on guiding their boat straight ahead. Apparently steering a boat was far more interesting than noticing the wildlife around him. With only a few boats visible, they almost had the lake to themselves.

It took about a half hour to reach the cove. Nick drove the boat up onto the rocky beach and killed the engine.

After the incessant roar of the motor, silence pressed in on her ears. Peaceful did not begin to describe the cove and the lush forest surrounding it.

Unbuckling her life jacket, Alisa left it on the seat before climbing out. Rags seemed the most happy to be rid of his encumbrance and shook himself from tail to nose.

They hauled everything out of the boat and carried their picnic to a sandy spot at the edge of the forest. Greg quickly found a stick, and the never ending game of fetch was on again.

Nick stood in the middle of the clearing, looking around. "Nice. Afghanistan was nothing but shades of brown. Rocks. Sand. Sun-scorched earth. Even what grass grew where I was stationed was covered with blowing sand that turned the blades dun colored."

He'd said so little about his time in Afghanistan, Alisa had a dozen questions she wanted to ask. What about the Afghani people? Were they friendly? And your fellow soldiers. What were they like?

With a shake of his head, he seemed to rid himself of the memories.

"So do we eat now or wait a bit?" he asked.

"Better let Greg run off some of his energy."

He spread the blanket next to a small embankment, sat down and pulled a can of soda from the ice chest. He leaned back with a sigh.

"A guy could get used to this."

"So could a girl. That's why my folks settled down here." Sitting down, she folded her legs and watched Nick as the tension in his face relaxed. A beautiful, rugged man at peace.

A pair of Steller's Jays landed nearby and began scolding them, pecking at the sand. One hopped up on the ice chest.

"That guy has seen ice chests before," Nick said. "He knows what's inside."

"If he could figure out how to open it, he'd probably help himself to the entire contents."

Nick chuckled and took another swig of cola.

"Oh, I forgot to tell you, Mama said she should be back by Friday."

"For a woman who hadn't ever taken a vacation, she sure sounds like she's making up for it now."

Alisa watched the jay hop to the ground and peck around in the sand. "I keep wondering if Mama and the doctor are, well, getting serious."

"Would that be a bad thing?"

"No, not really. I want her to be happy."

He eyed her over the top of his soda can. "Just kind of weird thinking about your mother having a boyfriend, huh?"

Soon Greg was ready to eat. Shooing off the jays, they downed the hard-boiled eggs she had made, ham sandwiches, chips and homemade cookies she'd baked in her upstairs kitchen. When Nick and Greg finished, they started tossing a football around. Alisa was ready to settle down to read her magazine, articles about keeping your man close to home and how to travel Europe as a single woman. Not that she had much chance to travel anywhere.

"Come on, princess." Nick reached down for her hand. "We're about to have a National Football League scrimmage. You're on Greg's team."

She eyed him skeptically as he pulled her to her feet. "Does it matter that I don't know much about football?"

"Naw. Greg'll teach you."

Alisa wasn't so sure.

Her first assignment was to hike the ball between her legs to Greg. It went clear over his head. Greg went running after it.

"You've gotta block me," Nick insisted.

"You're bigger than I am." She tried to get in front of Nick, but he easily danced around her to go after Greg.

"Run, honey!"

Nick caught up with Greg, lifted him in the air and set him down on the ground. All the while Greg laughed and screamed. "Not fair! Penalty!"

"Second down," Nick announced.

Greg and Alisa huddled. Greg decided he'd hike the ball to her and then block Nick.

The net result was about the same, except Nick picked Alisa up and carried her backward all the way to their end zone.

"Touch back! Two points for my team," he said softly as he put her down, his incredible blue-green eyes riveted on hers.

Her heart pounded against her ribs. Her mouth went dry, and she licked her lips.

"Come on, Nick," Greg interrupted. "I gotta kick the ball to you now."

Alisa stepped back. The game was on again.

When Nick was ahead by about fourteen-gazillion to nothing, Alisa cried uncle. Laughing, she collapsed on the blanket.

"I don't mean to complain, but I think the game was rigged," she said.

"You're right," Nick said as he stretched out beside her. "You outnumbered me two to one."

She gave him a playful punch on his shoulder.

Giving her a mischievous smile in return, he tucked his hands behind his head and looked up at the sky. Somewhere nearby a woodpecker beat a rapid rhythm in search of a morsel to eat. A sparrow sang a chirping song in response.

After a while, Alisa glanced out over the lake. She frowned and sat up straighter.

"Nick, a wind has come up. The lake's getting choppy."

He raised himself on one elbow. "Clouds coming from the west. We'd better get home before the storm gets here."

As much as Alisa might have liked being stranded on the beach with Nick, she agreed. She started packing up their things.

She didn't cherish the thought of riding in their twelve-foot open boat over rough, choppy water.

# *Chapter Fourteen*

Nick steered into the wind. Alisa was huddled down as low as she could get in the bow, her jacket up over her head, but she was getting drenched with the spray that flew up in front of them every time the boat bounced over a wave.

"Hang on tight, Greg," he warned. "This isn't a good time for a swim."

"I'm okay," the boy answered, grinning back over his shoulder. "I think this is great! It's like riding a bucking bronco."

The kid was fearless. A real trouper. He'd probably eat up a roller coaster ride. Nick had when he was a youngster.

Figuring out the situation for himself, Rags was hunkered down low in the middle of the boat. Unfortunately, a couple of inches of water had splashed into the boat giving the dog an icy-cold place to sit.

Chiding himself for not checking the latest weather report before they left Bear Lake, Nick had no choice but to keep going against the wind and chop. He'd get them all back to shore as fast as he could safely go.

The trip took twice as long it had taken that morning. By the time they got back to the municipal dock, everyone was soaked through. But they had beaten the storm back to the town of Bear Lake.

Nick got them into the truck, cranked the engine over and turned on the heater. He backed the truck and trailer into position on the ramp and hauled the boat out of the water, then secured the tie downs. By the time he got back into the truck, he was shivering and the cab smelled of wet dog.

"You're so cold you're shaking," Alisa pointed out unnecessarily.

"I'll warm up in a minute." Gritting his teeth, he drove out to the road and turned toward home. Not a terrific way to end what had been a great outing, putting them all at risk of pneumonia.

Still chilled when they got home, Alisa hefted the ice chest out of the pickup and hustled Greg inside while Nick moved the truck away from the door.

"I want you to go upstairs and get out of those wet clothes," she told Greg.

"I'm not very wet, Mom."

"Your pants are soaked, and the spray went right through your jacket. Go," she ordered. She should have known to dress Greg in more layers. Waterproof layers.

With heavy feet, Greg stomped upstairs. He tossed his jacket on the couch.

"Hang it up so it will dry, honey."

He did as asked, then flopped down on the couch. "Nick's a great guy, isn't he?" Longing seasoned his words.

"Your pants and shoes." She hung up her jacket to dry. "Yes, Nick is nice."

"It'd be great if he could stay here forever and ever."

She froze and eyed her son. "He may decide to leave. This isn't his home, you know." Even though this was where Nick was born and she wished he'd stick around, too.

"But he knows a lot of stuff, like fishing and painting stuff and football. If he stayed, he could teach me all that."

A lump formed in her throat, fear that her son wouldn't get his wish. Nor would she.

Sitting down next to her son, she picked up his foot and removed his shoe and his sopping wet sock. "It would be nice if he stayed. But that's going to be his choice, not ours. Besides there are lots of men in town who could teach you all those things."

His lower lip puffed out. "Not as good as Nick could."

Leaning down, she pulled off his other shoe and sock, and put them aside. She kissed his forehead, noting he smelled a lot like a wet dog.

"I love you, munchkin. You're growing up to be a fine young man."

Not wanting her son to see the tears that were forming in her eyes, she walked into her bedroom to change clothes. Too bad she couldn't alter her growing feelings for Nick as easily as putting on dry clothes.

In his room at the motel, Nick gave Rags a bath before cleaning himself up.

Rags still looked a little damp around the edges when it was time for Nick to get to work. He left Rags in the room and jogged the short distance to the diner.

The sky had darkened, and the air smelled of approaching rain. Wind tossed the tops of the fir trees back and forth like old ladies wagging their fingers at a misbehaving child.

Now that he'd finally warmed up, he felt good. Really good. Refreshed and freer than he'd been in a long while. If he could, he'd go on a picnic every day. With Alisa. Greg, too.

"Hey, Jake." He greeted the handyman who had returned to work and was sitting at a table in the back eating his dinner. "How's it going?"

Jake, a man in his sixties with a deeply tanned face, touched two fingers to his forehead in a salute. "Glad to be back. Spokane is too big for me."

"I hear ya." Nick grabbed a white jacket, slipped it on, then joined Hector at the prep table. He checked the orders to be filled. "We don't look too busy yet."

"The rain will keep the locals away. Tourists will still come. They've gotta eat."

"Right." Nick started on the day's cream of chicken soup, a pretty basic recipe but a popular item on the menu. On a chilly night like tonight, they'd get lots of orders for what could be a full meal, heavy on rich cream, light on spices.

He chopped up onions, carrots and celery, and dropped them into the pot to cook covered for a few minutes. While that was going on, he got bags of cooked, diced chicken breast from the refrigerator and broth from the pantry. As he worked, he hummed to himself.

Jolene put up an order for blackened steak penne, shrimp alfredo and a hamburger plate. Nick started on the pasta while Hector tossed steak, shrimp and two beef patties on the grill.

As he was working, Nick heard a distant rumble.

Tensing, he glanced up. Nothing to worry about. Just the storm coming.

He turned back to his work quickly. From the corner of his eye, he caught a reflection. Orange and red flames engulfing the room.

Squinting, he refocused on the boiling water, the pasta simmering in the steaming bubbles. *Nothing is happening. It's only a memory. You're safe.* He touched the rubber ball in his pocket but kept on working.

He plated the pasta, added alfredo sauce and passed the plate to Hector to add the shrimp. Then he did the same for the steak penne.

He reached for the next order. The flames had moved. They licked at the fragile slip of paper, scorching the corners.

*It's not real, Carbini. There is no fire!*

His hand trembling, he grabbed the order. He didn't get burned. Everything was okay.

Another rumble echoed outside.

An order for two bowls of chicken soup. Nick plucked up soup bowls from a stack behind him. He dipped the ladle into the pot. His vision blurred. Scenes from the past reappeared. The soup in the ladle seemed to change from creamy to blood red.

A scream lodged in his throat.

He dropped the ladle onto the counter. It rolled off onto the floor, spilling a red liquid that spread like blood over the tile floor. *Screams. Dying. Dead.*

A flash as bright as a floodlight lit the kitchen. The roar of a cannon followed on its heels. Alisa arrived to pick up the steak, shrimp and burger order. She put the dishes on a tray and hefted it on her shoulder.

Then another flash. Another boom. The lights went out.

In that last flash, Nick was transported back to Afghanistan and the outlying post which had been attacked.

"Incoming fire!" he screamed. "Down everybody. Get down!"

In the darkness, he saw the figure of one of his buddies. Still standing.

"Get down, Hank!" He dove for his friend. Knocked him down. Metal crashed around them. Dishes shattered. Burning chunks struck Nick's back. Ripped into his leg. Hank screamed, a high, shrill sound of pain. He'd been hurt. *Dear God in heaven, don't let him die!*

Hands grabbed him from behind. Insurgent hands. He fought the intruders but he wasn't going to let go of Hank. *Don't die, Hank. Don't die!*

After Nick tackled Alisa, sending the tray of orders flying, she screamed and struggled with him on top of her. Protecting her? But from what? The storm had knocked out the electricity. Nobody was going to die. Who on earth was Hank?

"Let go of me, Nick! Let go!"

"Keep down," he ordered. "They've overrun the defenses."

"Who's overrun what defenses?" She tried to flip him off of her body, but he held on tight. Too tight.

In the light from the emergency lamps, everything was cast an eerie shadows, turning ordinary objects into unfamiliar shapes. The blue-red glow of burners on the stove. Figures moving. Hector trying to pull Nick off of her.

"I've got you, Hank. Keep your head down." Nick shouted.

"Nick! What's happening?"

"He's gone crazy, Miz Alisa," Hector cried. "I can't hold him."

"Let go of me," Alisa repeated.

Her heart thundered in her chest. She fought back a building panic. "Someone get a flashlight."

Moments later, a tunnel of light swept the room and landed on Alisa. She squinted. Jolene had come to their rescue.

Alisa and Nick were a tangle of arms and legs, laying on the floor amid broken dishes and spilled food. Hector was trying to drag Nick away from the pile. When she wiped her hand across her forehead, she felt blood oozing from a cut.

Jolene stepped into the middle of the melee. "Nick! Let go of Alisa. What's gotten into you?"

"Get down! The insurgents are overrunning the camp!" His eyes were wide and wild, black as coal. "Has anybody got a gun? They're coming in the kitchen! Stop them!" A thunder clap shook the diner. "Grenade launchers. Get down!"

His flailing arm grazed Jolene's cheek.

Alisa feared for her safety and for Jolene's. It tasted bitter in her mouth. Knotted in her stomach. Weakened her knees. The reality of Nick's hallucination, the cause, slammed into her chest, taking her breath away.

"Nick. Look at me! I'm Alisa." She clamped her hands around his face. Creamy chicken soup had splashed all over him. Bits of wet pasta were stuck in his hair. "You're in Bear Lake. You're home. Not Afghanistan. You're safe. No one's trying to hurt you."

His thrashing slowed. He looked at her but without recognition.

"Let me go, Nick. I'm all right."

He relaxed his grip. Alisa sat up. Hector backed away.

"That's good, Nick. You're going to be fine now." Tentatively, she brushed the pasta from his hair.

"Hank?" His voice sounded bewildered. On the verge of tears.

She swallowed hard. "Hank's not here. You don't have to protect him anymore."

"Hank's my friend. He wanted to be a chef. Like me." Nick sat up, his knee bent. Looked around the darkened kitchen.

Whatever had happened in Afghanistan, Nick's wounds went far deeper than a titanium rod and a few screws in his damaged leg. They went soul deep.

"I know Hank's your friend. You took care of him as best you could. You were trying to keep me safe, too."

He shook his head. "No! I let him down. There was blood everywhere. I couldn't stop the bleeding."

"Shh, now," she crooned as she would to Greg if he'd been hurt. "It's going to be all right."

"Nooo," he sobbed, burying his head on his arm that he'd braced on his bent knee. His back shook as he made a terrible keening sound that sliced through Alisa's heart.

The overhead lights flickered then came fully on. Alisa looked around and found Hector standing nearby, his face pale.

"I don't know what happened. The lightning, thunder. The power went off." Hector shrugged helplessly. "Nick, he went a little crazy, I think."

More than a little, Alisa suspected. The memories that must have haunted him since the day he was wounded had flooded his brain with remembered terror. For Nick, the sudden darkness, the sounds of the storm, had been as real as though on a battlefield.

Jolene handed Alisa a towel, and she held it to her forehead. A red mark had appeared on Jolene's cheek. "Are you hurt?" Alisa asked.

"I don't think he meant to hurt me. It was just a wild swing."

Continuing to stroke the back of Nick's head, Alisa nodded. "He was trying to help his best friend in Afghanistan. I think he lost him in the war."

Alisa tried to think of what she should do first. "Hector, could you get the burners turned off and clean up this mess? We're going to have to close."

She glanced toward the swinging door where Tricia, a high school senior who worked part-time as a waitress, was standing looking aghast.

"Tricia, I need you to ask everyone out front to leave and lock up after them. Doggie bag whatever they want and no charge for any of the meals. Tell them there's been an accident in the kitchen."

"Yes, ma'am." After one last troubled look, Tricia turned to do as she'd been asked.

"Jolene, you're shaking. I want you to call your husband to pick you up. I don't want you driving home alone. Then would you please call Pastor Walker. Ask him if he could come over." She knew the pastor did some counseling at the VA clinic at Kalispell. Surely he'd know what to do.

Alisa hooked her arm under Nick's. "Come on, Nick. I'm going to take you upstairs. Get you cleaned up."

With an effort, he got to his feet. He shrugged her off like a drunk who wouldn't listen to reason, insisting he was all right to drive.

"I'm okay." Unsteady, he backed away. His gaze darted around the kitchen as though he wasn't sure where he was. "I don't need any help. Leave me alone." He backed all the way to the door, pushed it open and stepped out into the steadily falling rain.

Alisa followed him as far as the door. She watched him walk through the rain, still wearing his white chef's jacket, to the motel and climb the stairs. A moment later, the light came on in his room.

"Oh, Nick. Why didn't you tell me how troubled you really are?"

# *Chapter Fifteen*

Nick woke to a blistering headache, a mouth that tasted like burned feathers and a whining dog.

He opened one eye. Rags stared back at him, his eyes filled with accusation.

"What's wrong?" His voice slurred. He hadn't been having a nightmare. Rags would've been up in his face licking him silly if that was the case.

Rags whined again.

Slowly, Nick realized it was light outside. Morning. He was lying on top of the bed, fully clothed. With his white chef's jacket still on. And he didn't remember how he got there.

With an effort, he pushed himself up to a sitting position, planting his feet on the floor. He speared his fingers through his hair. Crazy images popped staccato fashion into his head, making the throbbing ache even worse: incoming rocket shells, Hank screaming, Alisa bleeding.

Rags went to the door and scratched it.

Someone knocked loudly enough that it made his headache worse.

He groaned. Unless the place was burning down, he didn't want to know who was on the other side of the door.

Whoever it was knocked again. "Nick, are you all right?"

*Alisa.* What could she want so early in the day? *Why had he seen her bleeding?* A dream. It had to have been a dream.

He staggered across the room and opened the door a crack. He squinted into the bright sunlight.

"What'd you want?"

"I was just checking to see if you were okay."

Except for the mother of all hangovers, he was fine.

His thoughts stumbled to a stop. He hadn't been drinking. There wasn't an ounce of booze in his room, and he sure hadn't gone out in that storm last night.

"Hang on a minute." He started to close the door, but she pushed it open.

Rags zipped out past her and ran down the stairs, his escape urgent.

"You slept in your clothes?" Alisa asked.

That seemed pretty obvious. It wasn't like he was dressed to go to work, not in this wrinkled mess. "I've gotta throw some water in my face."

In the bathroom, he locked the door. The water revived him to a point. But when he looked in the mirror, he saw a stranger. Heavy five-o'clock shadow. Red-rimmed eyes with dark rings beneath them. Hair that looked like someone had taken an egg beater to him.

That's pretty much how he felt all over.

He ran a brush through his hair. Gargled some mouthwash. Yanked off the white jacket and tossed it aside. For the moment, that was the best he could do.

Alisa was still standing in the middle of the room, the door wide open. In the sunlight, he noticed a bandage on her forehead. His stomach lurched.

"What happened to you?" he asked.

"It's nothing." She touched the bandage with her fingertips. "I was worried about you when you didn't come in for breakfast."

He glanced at his watch. After eight o'clock. He must have slept like the dead.

Images hopped-skipped through his head. Not Afghanistan. Here. The picnic. The race back home through wind-chopped waves. Starting the prep for dinner. Lightning. Thunder like the sound of a howitzer.

Memories slid into place. Explosions. Screaming. Blood.

Stumbling, he sat down hard on the end of the bed. "What did I do?"

"My guess is you had a really bad flashback."

"I hit you?" No, he couldn't have done that. He wouldn't have hit her.

"No, you tried to save me just liked you tried to save your friend Hank. The cut's from a broken piece of dinnerware. It's not your fault."

"Yeah, it is."

He buried his head in his hands. His worst nightmare. He'd been awake, yet the memories had driven him back to Afghanistan. He'd lost Hank all over again. His buddy's blood all over his hands. Blood and gore all around him. The rebels pounding the outpost with rocket-launched grenades and small arms fire. Turning his kitchen into a killing field.

Except this time Alisa had been the one injured.

He caught Alisa's floral scent, which brought him back to the present. She stroked the back of his head just as she'd caressed him last night. Soothed him. After he'd wrestled her violently to the floor. He'd vowed he would never be like his father. He'd never hurt a woman. Now he'd broken his own sacred promise.

"Why didn't you tell me you had PTSD?" She asked so softly, pain in her voice, that he could barely hear her.

He swallowed the boulders of guilt and regret.

They went down hard. “There isn’t anything you can do about it.”

“I called Pastor Walker last night. He came over but you wouldn’t open the door. You told him to go away.”

Nick didn’t remember that. He didn’t want to talk to the pastor. Or anyone else.

“He says you need to talk to someone. You can call him anytime. He has helped other veterans. Or you can talk to me. I’ll listen, Nick.” Her voice trembled. “Let me help you.”

“No.” He shot to his feet. “I’ve already hurt you once. You don’t want to be anywhere near me. I could lose control again. You aren’t safe around me. No one is.”

“That’s not true, Nick.” She reached for him. “You were being a hero, in Afghanistan and last night. It’s your nature.”

He turned her away from him. Pushed her toward the open door just as Rags trotted back into the room.

“Get out, Alisa. Leave me alone. No one can help me. I’m no hero. I’m dangerous.” He closed the door behind her.

Slowly he slid to the floor and curled up in a fetal position. God help him, he wanted to die. He should have died in Afghanistan with his men. Why hadn’t God taken him too?

Rags nudged him with his cold nose and licked

his face. This time it didn't rouse Nick from the waking nightmare that had dogged him all the way from a tiny outpost in a barren land to Bear Lake where his journey had begun.

Back at the diner, Alisa sat down alone at the old duffers' booth. She stared at the jigsaw puzzle. An English castle with crenellation on the battlement wall, parapets, arrow slits, a raised drawbridge over a moat.

That was like Nick, she reasoned. His pain was so great, he hid behind the battlements only occasionally allowing a glimpse of himself through a small arrow slit. Even when he let down his defenses, he admitted no one to the castle keep. Or to his heart.

A long siege was the one option that might succeed in getting him to lower the drawbridge. But Nick was too clever. He had a history of moving on before anyone could breach all the barriers he had erected.

This time would be no different.

She selected a puzzle piece, an iron-tipped spike in the portcullis meant to impale an enemy foolish enough to attack the castle, and slipped it into place. She could almost feel the spike being driven through her heart.

Ever since Nick arrived, she'd been building castles in the sky. Now the mortar was crumbling as she'd always known it would.

"Oh, Nick..." She covered her mouth with her hand. *Please don't hide in the castle keep. Let me in past the fortress you've built around yourself.*

Jolene, wearing street clothes, sat down opposite her. The bruise on her cheek had turned blue.

Alisa frowned. "You're not working the morning shift, are you?"

"I came in to find out how Nick is. And you."

Shaking her head, Alisa said, "I went to his room. He looks terrible."

"What happened wasn't that big a deal. Anybody can lose it sometimes."

"I don't think he feels that way about his flashbacks."

Jolene reached across the table to take Alisa's hand.

"You've fallen hard for him, haven't you?"

"Once a fool, always a fool."

"You're no fool, honey. And neither is Nick. There's more between you two than you give yourself credit for. He's crazy about you. Anybody can see that."

"I'm not so sure he can, and I'm scared to death he's going to leave. Become a drifter again." No telling how far he'd run this time, but Alisa knew if he left, he'd never come back. In time, she might be able to bear the pain. But what about Greg? Would he ever recover from such a loss?

Jolene squeezed her hand. "All we have to do is figure out a way to get him to stick around and get some help. He's not the first veteran to come home from a war with his head all messed up."

"So what do you suggest? Lock him in the tool-shed until he comes to his senses?"

Jolene's lips twitched into a smile. "That might be worth a try, but I'm not sure it would work."

Then what? Alisa wondered, picking up another puzzle tile. She didn't have a dungeon handy. And she didn't think starving him into loving her would be the answer.

She only knew that he was the best, most honorable man she'd ever met, a true hero, and she didn't want to lose him. That's exactly what would happen if he walked away now.

The only thing she could do was hope that somehow he'd recognize that Bear Lake was where he belonged before it was too late.

Nick didn't know how long he lay curled up on the floor. The lick of Rags's slobbery tongue and a soft whine roused him.

His limbs heavy with remorse, it took all of Nick's strength to stand up. Rags's tail started to wag as if he was the happiest dog in the world to see his master up and moving again.

"I'm sorry, Rags. Forgot about feeding you, didn't I?" He found Rags's dog food and opened a can, dumping the contents into his dish. He'd failed Rags along with everyone else. "It's time for us to move on, boy. I hurt her last night. I'm not going to risk hurting her again."

Then he took a shower. He let the hot water pound on his head full force until it turned icy cold. Shaved and dressed, he went downstairs. His leg hurt with each step he took. He hadn't put the boat trailer away when they'd returned from their picnic. Rags dogged his footsteps as though afraid he'd be left behind.

"I'm only putting the boat in the shed. No need to go nutso on me." Rags had been abandoned once. Maybe he still remembered being alone and hungry without his owners.

Climbing into the truck cab, he backed the trailer toward the shed. Jake Domino came out of the shed carrying a toolbox.

"Hey, Nick. You need some help?"

"No, I've got it." Just like he had his PTSD under control. Until he didn't anymore.

"Looks like you got some rainwater in the boat. We ought to drain that out before you put it away."

Jake was right, of course. Nick hadn't been thinking straight. Another residual problem of flashbacks.

Sniffing all around, Rags acted like he wanted to help, too.

"Stay clear, boy." Nick climbed up into the stern of the boat. A good three inches of lake water and rain had accumulated in the bottom of the boat. He reached down into the water to twist the drain plug. The old plastic handle broke off in his hand. Nick winced.

"That don't look good," Jake said.

No, it didn't. "Give me a hand. We'll tip the water out."

Nick loosened the stern tie down, Jake took care of the bow.

"Heard you had some problems in the kitchen last night," Jake said.

Nick froze, his hands wrapped tightly around the gunnel on his end of the boat. "Yeah, we did." He'd messed up big time.

"Lot of guys came back from 'Nam all messed up. Nobody knew what was wrong with 'em and didn't much care. I hear things are better now." Jake grabbed the gunnel in front of him. "Ready to roll her over?"

"Yeah." What Nick didn't like was everybody and his cousin knowing about his PTSD and acting like the cure was easy. "One, two, three…"

Together they rolled the boat up on its side until the water spilled out, nearly catching Rags in the waterfall. They lowered the boat back on to the trailer.

Jake peered over the side. “Looks like we’ll have to drill out that old drain plug and get a new one.”

*Great!* At this rate, Nick would never get out of town. “Does the general store have boating equipment?”

“Nope. Gotta go to either Kalispell or Polson. Polson’s closer.”

“Right.” Nick leaned his elbow on the frame. “Have you got time to drill out the plug? I’ll drive down to Polson.” He couldn’t leave the boat without a drain. Alisa might try to take the boat out on her own. Or Greg.

“Sure, I can do that.”

They tied down the boat again. Nick backed the boat into the shed and unhitched the trailer.

“I’ll be back as soon as I can.”

From the upstairs window, Alisa saw Nick’s truck pull out of the parking lot. She drew a painful breath. Was he leaving? Without saying goodbye?

With the crazy thought that she could stop him, Alisa ran downstairs. She burst out the kitchen door only to realize he was already gone. Breathing hard, she pressed her lips together. She never should have let her heart lead her head.

Rags leaped up on to the porch and nuzzled her. “Did he forget you?” That hardly seemed possible.

Nick loved Rags. In some ways, they'd been soul mates. Two lost souls.

Her hand idly petting Rags, she walked down the steps and stared up at Nick's room. Had he cleared out his things? Or was he coming back? Maybe he had an errand to run. Maybe to talk to Pastor Walker. She prayed that was the case.

The shed door was standing wide open. The buzzing of a drill drifted outside. Sounded like Jake was at work. She strolled inside and found him squatting in the stern of the fishing boat.

Jake stopped the drill, lifted his head and gave her a grin. "If you're lookin' for Nick, he's gone after a new drain plug for the boat in Polson. The handle on this one broke off."

The tension in her shoulders relaxed. "Thanks, Jake."

"He'll be back in an hour or two."

Back to stay? Or back only long enough to put in the new drain plug?

Nick stopped to get a burger in Polson before he headed back to Bear Lake with the new plug. He hadn't had breakfast, and his stomach had been rumbling.

Fortunately, being out on the road had cleared his head. It might be years before he stopped having flashbacks. No way could he stay anywhere permanently. He couldn't get involved with the lives of other people. The only safe recourse was to keep moving on.

The thought tightened in his gut. He tried to swallow his last bite of hamburger. It went down like a giant wad of cotton.

He reached Bear Lake and turned off the road at the diner, driving all the way back to the shed. Rags came trotting over to greet him. It stunned Nick that he'd left the dog behind and hadn't even tied him up.

"You sure picked the wrong master, boy," he said as he climbed out of the truck. If he could forget his dog in the haze of a flashback and its aftereffects, he could just as easily abandon Rags at a rest stop and not even remember he'd left the dog behind. Like Rags's prior owners had.

Rags deserved better than that.

Nobody was around, and it didn't take him long to install the new plug, even with Rags hanging only inches away from him as though he was afraid Nick would leave him again.

Going to his room in the motel, Nick packed his duffel bag, grabbed his bedroll and left his key card on the dresser. Better to make a clean break than go through a lingering goodbye.

Just as he tossed his duffel and bedroll into the truck, Greg arrived home from school. Rags raced over to greet the boy, giving him happy licks in the face.

"Hey, Nick. What're you doing?" Greg trotted over to the truck with Rags beside him.

Nick stalled, trying to figure out how to get away without telling the kid he wasn't coming back. But that didn't seem fair to Greg. The poor kid had been sucked into hero worship, which had been a bad idea from the start.

"I'm getting ready to leave," he said.

Greg's mouth dropped open and his eyes widened. "Where're you going?"

"I don't know. I'll drift awhile, see where I end up." Ending here in Bear Lake was a mistake. He'd hurt Alisa. He wasn't going to risk doing that again.

"When are you coming back?"

Nick rested his hand on the boy's shoulder. He tried to keep his voice steady. Sympathetic. But he wasn't too successful. "I'm…not coming back, son."

Tears glistened in Greg's blue eyes. "Are you taking Rags with you?"

Man, the kid really knew how to get to him. Tears. A trembling lower lip. His eyebrows flatlined.

"Actually, I was thinking…" Nick looked down at Rags and gave him a pet. His own eyes teared up and he cleared his throat. "I figured I'd leave Rags with you. I know you'd take good care of him."

"But you're not going to stay?"

"Nope. I can't." Every boy needed a pet to love. He could do that much for Greg.

"Why are you going? Don't you like me any-more?" His voice trembled.

"I like you a lot, buddy. But I did something real bad last night, and I hurt your mom."

The boy's eyes narrowed. "Did you do it on purpose?"

"No, it was an accident." He'd lost control, which was almost the same as hurting Alisa on purpose.

"Was Mom mad at you this morning?"

She should have been. "It doesn't matter. I've got to leave." What if he'd had a flashback and hurt Greg? Alisa would never forgive him for that.

"I don't want you to go!" Greg threw himself at Nick, wrapping his arms around him and held on tight.

Hesitantly Nick returned Greg's hug. "I have to, son."

"No, you don't!" His voice was muffled against Nick's chest. "You could stay here forever. Mom would let you."

Yeah, and she'd be a fool to do so. "I'm sorry, sport." Gently, he eased Greg's arms from around him. "Let's get Rags's leash. You can tie him up so he won't try to follow me. Then he'll be your dog."

"No!" Greg screamed. "I don't want Rags. I want you to stay here with me." Sobbing, he raced away toward the kitchen door.

Nick grabbed Rags before he could follow the boy, thinking it was a game of chase. "Come on, fella. You're gonna like it here much more than bumming around with me. Better chow and everything."

He tied the leash to the back porch railing, got the remaining cans of dog food out of the truck and piled them on the steps. "Stay, boy. Stay with Greg."

His footsteps hurried, he climbed into the truck. This was for the best, he told himself. Best for Greg and Alisa. That's what mattered.

Greg came flying upstairs screaming. "Mom! You gotta stop him. He's leaving."

Alisa leapt to her feet. Her heart raced. "What are you saying?"

"Nick's leaving. Right now." Greg's eyes were red-rimmed, tears streaming down his cheeks. His breath came in hard gulps. "Please, Mom. Stop him!"

Her heart sank into her stomach. "I don't think I can."

"You have to, Mom!" he wailed.

She could try. But after her talk with Nick this morning, she knew it would be an exercise in futility. And painful.

Greg thundered down the stairs ahead of her.

They burst outside. He stopped on the porch. "His truck's gone!"

Tied to the railing, Rags lunged at the length of his leash trying to follow Nick's truck that had just turned onto to the highway.

"Nick must be coming back," Alisa said. "He wouldn't leave Rags." He'd leave her and her son, but not his beloved dog. And then she spotted the cans of dog food.

"No, Nick said he wanted me to have Rags. But I want 'em both to stay!"

Heartsick for her son, Alisa didn't know what to say or do. Nick had made an enormous sacrifice by leaving Rags behind. If only he had asked for help, talked to Pastor Walker. Anyone. He might not have needed to leave.

One last lunge, and Rags broke free. He raced toward the highway to follow Nick's truck, four feet of leash flying out behind him like the tail of a kite.

"Rags, come!" she cried.

Greg took off after the dog. And Nick.

"Honey, come back. You can't catch him." She started running, too, but knew she'd never catch up with Greg until he ran out of gas. *Please, Lord, help me to help my son.*

Nick clamped his hands hard on the wheel. Tourist traffic was as heavy as midsummer. People gawking as they drove through town on a bright autumn day. Cars moving at the speed of desert tortoises.

At this rate, he'd never get out of town. Much less far enough away to forget Alisa and her son.

He clinched his jaw against the urge to give up. Go back. He'd made his decision.

Glancing in the rearview window, he frowned. A familiar-looking dog was racing along the side of the road. Not far behind him, he spotted Greg trying to catch up.

He wheeled off the road into the dirt. Of all the dumb, stupid… Why hadn't Rags stayed like he'd told him to?

Reaching across the cab, he popped open the door.

Rags leaped into the truck first. He came at Nick with his tail wagging and his lolling tongue.

Avoiding a face lick, Nick shoved him into the backseat. "I told you to stay," he said gruffly. Rags didn't appear the least contrite.

A long thirty seconds or so and Greg climbed into the cab, his face red from exertion, his chest heaving.

"What do you think you're doing?" Nick asked.

"Rags broke his leash."

Yeah, right. Maybe with a little help from Greg. *Or God?* That didn't make any sense. Why would

God be so all-fired anxious for him to stick around Bear Lake?

Now, however, Nick had no choice but to take the boy and his dog back to the diner and Alisa.

Dread filled his chest as he realized he'd have to explain himself.

## *Chapter Sixteen*

Alisa ran out of breath after less than a city block. Frantic to catch up with Greg, she slowed to a walk and kept going. An ache developed in her side. How far ahead of her was he? She'd lost sight of him.

She glanced at oncoming traffic and halted abruptly. Was that Nick's truck? White with a camper shell on the back. She couldn't be sure. There must be hundreds of pickups just like his.

She caught a glimpse of his dark hair and his profile. "Nick!" she screamed, waving to attract his attention. She started jogging toward him. "Nick! Do you have Greg?"

He glanced across the road in her direction and frowned. "I got him."

*Thank You, Lord!*

She continued to shadow Nick's truck as he drove back toward the diner. She caught a glimpse of Rags, his face pressed against the window, but she couldn't see her son. She had an urge to shake some sense into Greg. He should have known he couldn't catch up with Nick's truck.

But apparently he had.

Maybe she'd be better off to shake some sense into Nick.

He parked the truck by the kitchen door and climbed out. Greg came around from the other side of the truck. Rags stayed inside keeping a close eye on his master.

Rubbing her side, Alisa beckoned Greg to her. "You know that was a foolish thing you did, running after Rags."

Hanging his head, he scuffed the toe of his shoe in the dirt, kicking up puffs of dust. "I didn't want him to get lost."

"We'll talk about it later. Right now I want you to go upstairs and wait for me. You may have a snack if you want one. I have something to say to Nick."

Greg looked up at Nick as though seeking his permission to stay.

"Do what your mom says, sport." He cocked his head toward the door.

With a quick, mutinous look toward Alisa, Greg trudged up the steps and into the diner.

"I tied Rags up to the porch railing," Nick said. "I didn't expect him to get loose or Greg to come after him. Or me." A defensive note sharpened his words.

She folded her arms across her chest. "Did it even occur to you that if you had told me you were leaving, I could have prepared my son? Going off like that, running *away*—"

"I wasn't running away. I never promised I'd stay here forever." A muscle jumped in his jaw.

"By *running away* you've hurt my son. He'd begun to count on you as a friend." More like a father figure, but surely Nick had understood what was happening. He should have understood what was happening between her and Nick as well, if he'd had any sense. Apparently, if he did recognize her growing feelings, it didn't matter to him. "Friends don't do that to friends. They explain things. They don't go off without saying goodbye."

"I did explain to Greg. I told him I'd hurt you. I had to leave."

"You had a flashback. You couldn't help yourself."

"Which is exactly why I'm leaving." He ordered Rags out of the truck and unhooked the trailing leash. "I want Greg to have Rags."

"You love that dog, and you're going to leave him?" Her voice rose incredulously. Did love mean so little to him? "Don't you know it will break his heart if you leave without him?" Just as it was breaking her heart now. She rubbed the heel of her palm against her chest as though she could ease the pain.

"It's better for him to stay here."

"He'll try to come after you again."

"Then tie him up good." He started to climb up into the truck, but Rags scooted past him and jumped in first, hopping into the backseat.

Nick mumbled something under his breath.

Behind Alisa, the kitchen door opened. Hector stepped out on to the porch.

"It's time to start the prep for dinner," he said. "Do you want me to start the dumplings?"

*The Thursday night special.* Hector had never managed to make perfect dumplings no matter how many times Mama had showed him her technique.

Alisa met Nick's gaze and held it. "No, Hector. I'll make the dumplings tonight," she said.

His dark brows tugged together. "I thought you hadn't mastered the technique."

"I haven't, but what other choice do I have except to cancel the special for tonight? Our customers would love that, wouldn't they?" She'd have a small riot on her hands. "It would be hard to explain our regular chef took off without notice." Her tone challenged him.

He jammed his hands in his jeans pockets. "You said Mama was coming back tomorrow?"

"Yes." She held her breath. She could almost see the wheels churning in his brain as he tried to think of an excuse to leave now. Or decide to wait one more day.

"You know if I go back in there, in the kitchen, I could have another flashback. Someone could get hurt again."

"You've been cooking in the kitchen for more than a week without having a problem."

"Sometimes I see things. On the stainless steel equipment. Reflections of the attack that hit our outpost."

He visibly shuddered, and Alisa's heart went out to him. He'd been fighting those memories for years and they still had an unbreakable grip on him. If he'd told her, maybe they could have done something. Put curtains over the refrigerator doors. Painted everything a dull black. He'd carried so many burdens. An abusive father. A mother who died young. Injured in the war. No wonder he hadn't learned how to ask or receive help. He felt he had to stand strong on his own. He'd been doing it for thirty years.

"Don't you think it was the storm, the thunder and lightning, that set you off?" she asked. "The weatherman isn't predicting another storm tonight."

He turned around and braced his outstretched arms against the hood of the truck. His head dipped.

"Okay, I'll try. I'll stay 'til Mama gets home, but then I'm gone." He turned back to her, his eyes bleak. "Do you understand? I can't take the risk of staying here any longer."

Alisa did understand. She had twenty-four hours to get him to change his mind.

And the same amount of time to prepare Greg for Nick's departure if she failed.

Nick's gut tightened into a knot as he dragged Rags out of the truck and used his old rope to tie the dog to the porch railing. He didn't know which had been harder, seeing Greg's broken hearted expression when Nick had told him he was leaving. Or being hammered by Alisa.

A hammering he deserved.

The last thing he wanted to do was step back into that kitchen where every reflective surface could bring back memories. Yet if he didn't get in there to prepare the chicken and dumplings for the special, he'd be letting Alisa down. And Mama.

Maybe he'd be letting himself down, too.

Chances were good it wouldn't be any easier to leave tomorrow than it had been today. Greg would still be upset. Alisa mad.

He stood on the porch for a long time before he built up the nerve to open the door. His heart was pounding hard when he stepped inside.

Without looking around the kitchen, keeping his eyes averted from the stainless steel surfaces, he grabbed a white jacket from the fresh linens and washed his hands at the sink.

"You okay?" Hector asked, eyeing Nick with some apprehension.

"Fine." If you called being crazy fine.

He tensed as he retrieved the milk from the refrigerator for the dumplings, trying hard not to focus on any reflections that might appear. The flour was easier. But then he had to work at the prep table that was polished to a high sheen.

*You've been doing it for more than a week, Carbini. Nothing's going to leap out and grab you now.*

Unless another thunder and lightning storm roared through the Bear Lake valley again.

The big pots of water rose to a rapid boil. He mixed up the dough for the dumplings and got out a supply of quarter chickens, thighs and drumsticks. A container of sour cream. The aroma of paprika and garlic began to soothe him. Good seasonings could do that. He'd learned that in his mother's kitchen.

He was finally getting into the rhythm when Alisa walked into the kitchen, dressed in her usual slacks and white blouse for work. She probably wanted to see if he'd wrestled anyone to the floor lately.

"How's it going?" Her furrowed forehead indicated she wasn't sure what his answer would be.

"Your customers will be satisfied with the special tonight."

"I really appreciate you staying. I know it's hard for you."

"Mama will be home tomorrow."

"Yes." Unable to hold his gaze, she glanced away. "If you feel another flashback coming on, tell Hector to come get me. I'll understand if you have to step outside away from all this." She gestured vaguely toward the stainless appliances.

"I don't usually get much notice. It just happens." Like being hit by a ton of bricks. Or a rocket-propelled grenade.

"I understand." She backed away by a couple of steps. "The crowd is beginning to pick up. I'd better get out there and help Jolene and Tricia."

"Sure. Go ahead. I'll try not to tackle anyone tonight or knock over a dinner tray."

Her lips pressed together, she shook her head from side to side before pushing her way through the swinging doors into the diner.

She'd said she understood, but Nick knew better. No one who hadn't experienced the terror of flashbacks could possibly understand the horror of reliving, time and time again, the fear that immobilized him.

The knowledge that he'd been a coward.

Nick was cleaning up the stove at the end of the shift when Alisa walked into the kitchen.

"Nick, let Hector finish the cleanup," she said. "There are some people out front who want to talk to you."

His head came up and he frowned. "I thought you'd closed up."

"This is something a little special."

Not at all sure what she was up to, and suspecting it wasn't anything he wanted, Nick set aside his cleaning rag and took off his jacket. He tossed it in the linen bin and followed her.

The lights were turned down low in the main part of the diner, and the Closed sign was on the door. Alisa led Nick into the banquet room. To Nick's dismay, Pastor Walker, Ned Turner, Ward Cummings and Mac McDonnell stood when they entered.

Nick stopped abruptly. He didn't like the look of this. "What's going on? If this is supposed to be a surprise birthday party, you've got the wrong date."

The pastor stepped forward. "This is what's called an intervention. Come, sit down, Nick. You're among friends here." His hand on Nick's shoulder, Walker urged him toward the table where they'd all been sitting. "Alisa, under the circumstances, I think you should stay, too."

A sense of anger building, Nick sat at the head of the table as he'd been told. *An intervention?* It looked more like *interfering* to him.

A coffeepot and mugs for everyone were on the table. Alisa filled a mug for him.

"I don't know what you're up to." He gave the men a hard stare. "I'll admit to being an alcoholic, but I haven't had a drop of alcohol in four years. I don't need an intervention." That's what families did when an alcoholic or drug addict wouldn't admit he had a problem.

"This is a different kind of an intervention, son." Walker sat next to Nick and gestured for Alisa to take the seat across from him. The other men settled into their chairs. "All of us are worried about you and how you're handling your PTSD."

Nick narrowed his eyes, the muscles in his throat flexed and he placed his palms flat on the table. The urge to flee—or start a free-for-all—churned through him. He fisted his hands.

"I'm handling it fine." He lifted one corner of his lip in warning. He wasn't going to put up with a bunch of near strangers telling him how to manage his flashbacks. Nothing had helped him so far.

"Are you handling it?" the pastor asked mildly.

"Yeah. Now can I go?"

"We heard you had a flashback last night," Ward said. "That doesn't sound like you're handling anything."

Nick shot an accusatory gaze in Alisa's direction for blabbing about him all over town. She didn't even blink.

"How 'bout nightmares?" Mac asked. "My wife still has to wake me up a couple of times a month."

"This stuff is none of your business," he said. "I'm leaving tomorrow and you won't have to worry about me again."

Walker covered Nick's hand with his. "All these men have been through situations similar to yours. They've worked through the trauma—some still are." He gave a nod to Mac. "You can, too, if you'll give us a chance to help."

Nick shot a look at each of the men. "The VA wouldn't give me the time of day. Said I could maybe have an appointment in like six months, assuming I wasn't malingering."

"We're here now, sergeant," Ned said. "Don't turn your back on us. We've been there."

For some reason, knowing Ned had suffered from PTSD, caused him to relax a little. But he still wanted out of there. Wanted them to leave him alone.

"I'm a cook, a trained chef," Nick said. "Cooks aren't supposed to get shot at. They aren't supposed to get PTSD."

"But you were and you did. Tell us what happened. That'll be a start." Walker nodded to encourage Nick to recall the memories that he'd been fighting for so long.

He wasn't sure he could do that, relive the whole thing again. But he saw nothing but sympathy in their eyes, Ted and Ward and Mac. They'd understand.

Alisa seemed to be holding her breath. Could she possibly grasp what it was like to be in a firefight?

Despite his reluctance, Nick took a chance and began to talk. The words, the memories, were hard at first. Like bayonets piercing his protective shield.

As he got further into his story, the images came back to him. His voice shook with the same terror he'd experienced more than four years ago. The inability of his unarmed crew to protect themselves. The sight of body parts blown into the air. Blood spraying on every surface, tainting his kitchen with death.

Vaguely he became aware his cheeks were damp with tears and he wondered when that had happened.

As he came near the end of the tale, he said, "I was a coward. I should've protected my men or died with them." He swallowed hard, his Adam's apple bouncing. "Instead I crawled on my belly into the big walk-in refrigerator and locked myself in. I don't know how long I stayed in there after it got all quiet. When I crawled out, they were all dead. I should've stayed with them."

Silent tears cascaded down Alisa's cheek. She squeezed his hand. "You survived, Nick. That's what's important."

He shook his head, knowing he could never accept that as the truth. He'd left them all there on the floor, dead or dying.

"That's good, Nick," the pastor said. "Is that the first time you've told anyone the whole story?"

He wiped the back of his hand across his face. "Yeah, I guess." Even in prison, when the chaplain had encouraged the guys to talk, he'd held back. Hadn't told them he'd been a coward.

All the fight and anger had gone out of him, and he lowered his head. Alisa's hand looked so small and delicate compared to his. She needed someone to protect her. Not a coward who crawled away when faced with danger.

Ned spoke up. "I used to blame myself for losing my whole squad. The thing is, there hadn't been any way I could have stopped the Vietcong from attacking us. We were outnumbered and surrounded."

"What could you have done, Nick, to stop the attack or protect your men?" The pastor posed the question in an understanding yet probing way.

"I don't know."

"None of you were armed?" he persisted.

"We'd all been issued M16s. We kept them in our barracks. I should've made them carry them every place they went."

"Last time I heard," Ward said, "an M16 wasn't effective against rocket-propelled grenades."

"They might have given us a chance," Nick countered. "Hiding in the refrigerator sure didn't help."

"You tried to help Hank, didn't you?" Alisa asked, her eyes pleading with him.

"He died. They all did." Accepting the blame stood like a stone wall, keeping these men at a distance. Alisa, too. That's what a coward deserved.

Lifting her chin, Alisa tried to stare him down with her compelling blue eyes, make him listen. "I don't believe for a minute what you did was cowardly, Nick Carbini. And neither do these men who care about you. You have to quit blaming yourself. You have to let them help you."

He didn't flinch. He simply stared back at her and steeled his emotions. "You're wrong, Alisa. Dead wrong."

Pushing his chair back, he stood.

Pastor Walker did, too. "You know where to find me, Nick. Call when you're ready to talk."

Nick left the room without saying another word.

## *Chapter Seventeen*

Alisa sat down with Greg at the kitchen table in the family quarters. Dressed for school, he'd fixed his own cereal and poured himself a large glass of orange juice.

"I need to talk to you, kiddo," she said.

He stuffed a spoonful of cereal in his mouth. "Okay."

"You know, instead of Nick leaving yesterday as he'd planned, he stayed around so he could make Mama's special chicken and dumplings for our customers last night."

Pretending disinterest, Greg focused on consuming his cereal. Milk dribbled down his chin, and he wiped it away with his shirt sleeve.

"Mama's coming back today."

The boy finally looked up. "I miss Mama. She's cool."

Alisa grinned. "I think so too." She could also

use some of Mama's wisdom right about now. Some way to ease her son's pain when Nick leaves. And her own broken heart. "Nick told me yesterday that he'd only stay until Mama gets home. That means he'll probably leave, possibly before you get back from school."

Another bite of cereal. A gulp of milk. A twitch of his shoulders. "I don't care."

"I'm sure you do care, honey." She put her hand on his shoulder, rubbing gently. "I'm sorry he's leaving, too, but we'll be all right. We're family. You, me and Mama." She fought the tremble in her voice. "He may decide to leave Rags with you. If he does, I think we can build a run for Rags back by the shed and a doghouse—"

Greg threw down his spoon and jumped to his feet. "I don't want Nick to stay, and I don't want his dog. Rags will just try to go after him again. And he'll get hit by a car and run over." Angry tears filled Greg's eyes. "Rags doesn't want to stay with me. Nobody does." He raced toward the stairs.

Leaping to her feet, Alisa ran after him."That's not true, Greg. Come back. We can talk..." She hurried down the stairs.

Billy Newton, the short-order cook, was at the stove preparing breakfast orders. He looked up as Alisa burst into the kitchen, but she ignored him.

She was too late. Greg was out the door before she got there, running as fast as his young legs could take him. Running away from his pain and loss.

Nick and her son were alike. Both running away rather than facing the truth. She could forgive Greg. He was only nine years old. Nick should know better.

Instead of sitting at the counter for breakfast where he'd likely have to deal with Alisa one-on-one, Nick headed to the old duffers' table. Two old guys were sitting there lingering over their breakfast coffee.

"You got room for another puzzle afficionado?" he asked.

In unison, two pairs of gray eyebrows rose.

"Sure. Sit yourself down," the older of the two said. "I'm Ezra Cummings. This here is Abe Packett."

Scooting a puzzle shape into place, Nick introduced himself.

"The Carbini boy, huh?" Abe, whose hands looked like baseball mitts, eyed him curiously. "I knew your old man, Sam Carbini. Worked at the mill, didn't he?"

"When he was sober." Small towns had long memories. Maybe too long.

"Yep, that's the one." Abe lifted his mug to his

lips. “I remember your mama, too. Nice lady.” He sipped his coffee. “Felt right sorry when I heard she’d passed on.”

Nick’s throat constricted, and he was grateful Jolene showed up right then with a fresh mug of coffee for him, ready to take his order.

“You want your usual eggs and toast?” she asked.

He cleared his throat. His mother used to make him pancakes…when they had enough money to buy milk. She picked wild blackberries in the fall to put on top.

“Let’s go for the wild side this morning. Ask Billy to cook up a couple of pancakes with blackberries on top, if he’s got any, and two eggs sunny side up.”

“You got it.” She checked with Abe and Ezra, who were good with their coffee, before going to the back to place Nick’s order.

Ezra reached across the table to pick up a puzzle piece. “Heard you been cooking the chicken and dumplings while Mama’s gone.”

“That’s true.” Nick studied Ezra’s selection, but couldn’t see where he was going to put it. This was one of those challenging puzzles with crazy geometric patterns that were tough to figure out. So far the old duffers had only gotten three-quarters of the border put together.

"We're right fond of Alisa and her mama. The boy, too." He tried to fit the piece in near the top border. It didn't match up. "We're all sort of family around here."

Picking up another piece, Nick wondered if he was hearing the hint of a threat: Don't mess with our friends. He slid the piece into place.

Ezra grunted.

Abe said, "You planning to stay around long?"

Nick decided he should've risked sitting at the counter. "Nope."

"Alisa know that?"

Leaning back in the booth, Nick gave the two men a hard stare. "She knows."

They both grunted, then leaned forward to find new pieces to stick in the puzzle.

Nick felt like he'd been kicked in the ribs. He deserved it. His leaving was going to hurt Alisa. Greg too. But what could he do? He'd hurt them a lot worse if he stuck around and had another flashback like the one the other night.

These old guys didn't know what he'd done, tackling Alisa to the floor, injuring her, or they'd probably run him out town.

No need for that. He'd be leaving under his own power as soon as Mama showed up.

When the pancakes arrived, they tasted like sawdust. The berries bitter on his tongue.

Memories were just that. You couldn't go back.

* * *

It was midafternoon when Mama showed up in Dr. McCandless's SUV. He pulled into a spot right in front of the diner.

From behind the counter, Alisa spotted them.

She stopped what she was doing and ran out to greet her mother. "Mama!"

The doctor helped Mama out of the car, and Alisa stepped into her mother's welcoming arms. "I'm so glad you're home," she said, surprised by the tears that formed in her eyes. Mama seemed to have shrunk while she'd been gone, not as tall as Alisa remembered and with more wrinkles, while before she'd always seemed bigger than life. Youthful. Maybe she'd always seen her mother through the eyes of her childhood.

"I'm glad to be home, too, *Alisova*." Stepping back to look at her daughter, Mama cupped Alisa's cheek. "What happened to your head?"

Alisa had all but forgotten she had a bandage on her forehead. "We had a little accident in the kitchen. It's nothing, really."

Mama's brows lifted, questioning.

"Let's get you inside." Avoiding her question, Alisa took one of the suitcases that Dr. McCandless had retrieved from the back of the SUV. "I'm sure you must be tired from the long ride."

"Not at all." Mama smiled fondly at the doctor.

"Oh, well...do come inside. I'm sure everyone will be happy to see you home safe."

Inside, Jolene was the first to greet Mama with a hug. "How was your trip?"

"Quite wonderful. We had an excellent tour guide and bus driver. He arranged it so we saw all the sights, at least those that didn't require hiking for miles into the wilderness." Mama laughed. "Half of us even took Jeep tours into the back-country."

"How wonderful for you," Jolene crooned.

A couple of their regulars greeted Mama, welcoming her home. They chatted for a bit before letting Mama proceed. Alisa thought sure Mama would want to go upstairs. Instead, she went right into the kitchen where Nick was prepping for dinner.

Mama beamed at him. "Nick! You're still hard at work I see."

"Welcome home, Mama." He wiped his hands on a cloth while Hector greeted her as well.

She turned back to Nick. "I hear you've had some good ideas to cut costs for us." She scanned the room to check that everything was in order.

"Alisa and I talked about a few things. She's waiting to go over them with you."

"Nick has already negotiated a better deal with the wholesaler by buying in bulk," Alisa said.

"Excellent." Glancing over her shoulder, she

smiled at the doctor. "Nick, it seems, is quite a good businessman."

McCandless smiled indulgently. "Glad to hear it."

"How are your burns?" Nick asked, his tone far more serious than Mama's had been, and Alisa suspected he was checking to see if he'd be free to leave.

Mama held out her hands, which still looked red and raw. "Royce can be a very bossy doctor. Medicine all the time. Exercises." She flexed her fingers. "Never giving me a moment's rest."

"Which has speeded your recovery, my dear," the doctor pointed out. "And remember, you must continue using the cream on your hands and arms, and doing your exercises."

Mama wrinkled her nose, but she didn't appear upset by the doctor's orders.

Greg came in the back door, his hair mussed from a day at school, saw Mama and ran to her. The routine of welcome home greetings and hugs continued until Mama decided she was ready to go upstairs.

Eagerly, without so much as a look in Nick's direction, Greg took Mama's smaller suitcase and followed Mama and the doctor upstairs.

Alisa's feet stayed rooted in place, the width of the prep table between her and Nick. She held her breath. Was he going to pack up and leave right now?

"Mama looks well rested," he said. "The trip must've been good for her."

"I suppose."

He picked up a wooden spoon to stir the potato pancake batter he'd been mixing. "I'll work through the dinner shift. Mama probably needs to rest. Then I'll leave in the morning."

Her spine rigid, her jaw tight, Alisa said, "I'll figure out what we owe you and get you the cash tonight before you leave."

His lips flattened into a straight line. "There's no need. I've got plenty of money."

"The Machaks always pay what we owe. And by the way, Greg says he doesn't want your dog."

She turned and walked upstairs to help her mother unpack. This time she'd be strong. She'd build a wall around her heart that no man would ever again scale.

After cleaning up the kitchen, Nick had requisitioned a couple of day-old sweet rolls from the diner to have for breakfast the next morning, and he'd made coffee in his room. He intended to slip away as unnoticed as possible. He'd said everything to Alisa that he needed to.

Guilt twisted in his gut. The wad of cash Alisa

had given him burned through his wallet in his hip pocket.

He hadn't said goodbye to Mama. She had hired him. Given him a chance when she didn't even know him.

He brushed the crumbs off the desk he'd used for a table and dumped the remaining coffee down the sink.

Mama should be grateful he was leaving before he hurt someone else during one of his flashbacks.

Rags sniffed at the crumbs that had landed on the carpet. "Come on, buddy. You already had your breakfast."

Picking up his duffel, he slung it over his shoulder. He felt bad about Greg not wanting to keep Rags. The boy should have a dog. And Rags needed a boy like Greg to play chase and fetch with, both of them expending all that irrepressible energy.

Downstairs, Nick tossed the duffel in the back of the truck and closed the tailgate.

He sat behind the wheel for a minute looking up at the window of the family quarters. A band tightened around his chest. No matter how he felt about Alisa, no matter how much he'd come to care, leaving was the best thing he could do for her.

Starting the truck, he drove out of the parking lot. Rags put his nose right up against Nick's neck and whined.

Nick patted the dog's muzzle. "We'll be okay, boy," he promised, although he was pretty sure that was a lie. "We've got lots of miles to travel today." But could he go far enough to forget Alisa's sweet floral scent or how her eyes lit up when she smiled? Or the way she'd tasted when he'd kissed her?

The first thing he did was stop at the gas station in town to fill up. For a long trip, he wanted to start with a full tank.

When he pulled out of the station, he turned right on to a residential road. He wasn't sure why he'd done that. But a couple of blocks later, he slowed to a stop across from the house where he'd been born.

A young mother was playing catch in the front yard with her toddler son. She'd toss a big beach ball to him. He'd try valiantly to catch it, usually falling down on his diapered butt. Up he'd get, chasing after the ball and throwing it back to his mom. Sort of.

"Good boy!" she cried when she scooped it up. "Just look at you. You're getting so big. Daddy thinks you're going to be a football player. How'd that be?"

The youngster laughed as though her comment had been the most uproariously funny thing anyone had ever said and clapped his hands.

"Okay, Bobby, here it comes again. Get ready." Mom tossed the ball and the whole scene repeated.

Unaccountably, tears burned at the back of Nick's eyes. Had his mother played with him like that? He couldn't remember being that young. But he did remember her walking him to the school bus on the first day of kindergarten. He'd been scared spitless.

She'd knelt beside him, handing him his lunch sack. She'd been so pretty, fair complexion, dark expressive eyes and hair as black and shiny as the ravens that cawed from the treetops. "Don't you worry, Nicky. You're going to be the smartest, most wonderful boy in your whole class. Your teacher is going to love you. If you have a problem, you just ask for help, okay?"

He remembered the dread in his stomach as he climbed into the bus. The fear he was going to throw up. All those bigger kids terrified him.

He'd headed for the back of the bus, got up on his knees so he could look out the window. His mom waved and threw a kiss as the bus pulled away. She'd gotten smaller and smaller until the bus turned the corner.

Somehow he'd found the courage to sit down and face forward. If he was going to be the smartest, most wonderful boy in his whole kindergarten class, he'd have to act it. Make his mom proud of him.

Wiping his tears away, he doubted his mother would be proud of him now. *Running away from his problems.*

In his head, he heard her sweet, loving voice again. “If you have a problem, ask for help.”

Almost like an echo, he heard Alisa at the intervention pleading with him. “You have to let them help you.”

He rested his head on the steering wheel. Maybe it was time to make his mother proud of him again. And Alisa.

# *Chapter Eighteen*

Alisa helped her mother prepare dinners for the Saturday night crowd. Mama wore soft, white-cotton gloves while she worked. Even so, Alisa could tell it hurt Mama to grasp the handles of pots and pans; she often used both hands to hold the weight.

Gritting her teeth, Alisa knew Mama's burns hadn't healed enough for her to be back to work, no matter what Dr. McCandless said. If Nick had cared about Mama, he would've stayed another couple of weeks.

Instead, he'd been so wrapped up in his problems, he'd run away. Talk about an egotist!

She plucked a medium-rare T-bone steak from the grill and slapped it on a plate, passing it to Hector to add the baked potato and veggies. Whatever Nick Carbini thought, the world did not revolve around him.

"You shouldn't have let him go." Mama serenely

scooped penne from a pan of boiling water, drained the noodles and covered them with a ladle of chicken in cream sauce with pesto. She added a dash of parmesan.

Alisa didn't pretend to not know who she was talking about, although her mother's words hurt. "How would I have stopped him? He was a drifter before he got here. He'll always be a drifter."

"If you had cared enough, Ben might have stayed."

"I cared." She plated a medium-well sirloin. "At least I thought I did." She'd certainly cried enough crocodile tears. Admittedly, some of those tears were from hormones due to her pregnancy. And fear, she supposed.

"I've seen the way Nick looks at you. Nick will come back, *Alisova.* And when he does, don't let him get away again."

Alisa snorted an unladylike sound. Maybe when she was old and gray Nick would return but not before. She didn't dare hope for even that. What good would it do anyway?

They worked side by side until the orders began to let up and the hum of voices from the diner quieted.

"Mama, I can handle things for the rest of the shift. You should go upstairs, get to bed early. You've put in a long day."

Looking tired, beads of sweat glistening at her

hairline, Mama set her stirring spoon aside. Wincing, she tugged off her gloves.

"I hate to admit it, but I am tired. If you're sure you and Hector can handle—"

"We'll be fine, Mama. You go ahead. You'll be stronger tomorrow." But what about the next day and the day after that? She wasn't getting any younger. Working as hard as she had all these years, soon she wouldn't be able to keep up the pace. Alisa would have to take over more and more of the load.

Not that she would mind. The Pine Tree Diner was the only home she'd ever known. In Bear Lake she was surrounded by friends who were like her family.

Her chin trembling, her eyes burning, she reached for the next order to be filled. Grilled chicken with dijon sauce and fresh trout rolled in cornmeal, fried in butter.

She turned to the refrigerator to get the chicken and trout. A tear leaked down her cheek. What she didn't have here in Bear Lake was a man to love who loved her in return. A man whose kisses made her feel like a woman.

Nick pulled his truck past the Pine Tree Diner to the back of the lot. It was past closing time. There were no cars around except those at the motel.

The kitchen was dark. So were the family quarters upstairs.

It had taken all the courage he had to come here after his hours-long talk with Pastor Walker. It was going to take even more chutzpah to talk to Alisa.

As likely as not, she could tell him to get lost. He wouldn't blame her.

The pastor had kept saying "Trust in the Lord." Nick would have to do that because he sure didn't think he was worthy of a woman as good and fine as Alisa.

But he was going to do his best to become that man.

Leaving Rags in the truck, Nick climbed out, picked up a few pebbles and walked toward the diner. It had begun to rain, splattering on the ground in big drops. He took a deep breath.

"I sure hope the pastor was right, Lord. If not, I'm likely to get a flowerpot dumped on my head."

Fingering a pebble, he tossed it at the living room window of the family quarters.

Unable to drop off to sleep, Alisa considered getting up to work on the jigsaw puzzle on the kitchen table. The mindless task would relax her. Quiet the riotous, what-if thoughts of Nick that were keeping her awake. The thought that if she had asked him to stay, told him that she loved him, he wouldn't have left.

Or, more likely, his rejection would have left her feeling more like a fool than ever.

She heard something *plink* against the living room window. Probably a big moth or a starling confused by the security lights outside.

Two more *plinks.* Apparently not a real smart moth.

A few more *plinks* and she was convinced there was a moth invasion outside the diner. Maybe locusts.

Climbing out of bed, she pulled her light robe around her and went into the living room. She opened the drapes. No moths or any other creatures she could see.

Something hit the window again and she jumped back. “What in the world?”

Cautiously, she approached the window and looked down at the ground. She gasped and her heart rate kicked up a notch. Nick? Standing there throwing something at her window? She’d thought he’d be hundreds of miles away by now.

*Nick will come back, Alisova.*

But for how long?

Opening the window, she stuck her head out. “What are you doing here?”

“I need to talk to you.”

Talk? His actions had done all the talking she’d wanted to hear when he drove away this morning.

“Can I come in?” His dark hair glistened with

raindrops. "I'm getting pretty wet out here. I promise I won't stay long."

Only long enough to break her heart. Again.

She didn't rush downstairs. It wasn't that she was playing hard to get. Her knees had gone all wobbly on a thin thread of hope. She'd really feel foolish if she tumbled down the stairs and broke something.

Cautiously, she opened the back door. He stood on the porch, the shoulders of his army jacket damp, his dark whiskers shadowing his square jaw. He looked like a hero home from the war and not knowing where he fit into civilian life or if he ever could. How had she not recognized that look the first day when he volunteered to chop kindling for her?

How had she not realized his drinking and fighting, his time in prison, had all been a result of his PTSD?

"Hi," he said in his low baritone voice.

"Hi, yourself." Opening the door wide, she stepped back to let him enter. She resisted the urge to grab him and hold on to him for fear she might never let him go. Or at least smooth his damp hair away from his forehead. But she couldn't do that either. "Is Rags with you?"

"In the truck. He's okay." He walked into the kitchen. The glow of the pilot lights on the stoves and the reflection of the outside security lights cast the room in phantom shadows. "I hope I didn't wake you."

"No, I wasn't asleep." *I was awake thinking of you.*

He shoved the lock of hair away from his forehead and shuffled his feet. "I was leaving town this morning, probably for good."

She swallowed hard. "I know."

"But for some reason, I drove by the house where I was born. Figured I'd take one last look, I guess. I sat there a long time watching a young mother playing with her son. It made me think of my mother. She was a good mom. I think you would've liked her."

"I'm sure I would have." Although Alisa wished Nick's mother could have protected him from his father. Perhaps she did until she died.

"You're a lot like her, you know?"

"That's nice of you to say." She wrapped her arms around herself against the chill night air. "Is that what you wanted to tell me?"

"Not exactly. The fact is, I started remembering how much I wanted her to be proud of me. And how I want you to be proud of me, too."

He was looking at her with such intensity, her breath hitched in her lungs.

"I spent most of the day talking to Pastor Walker." He took a deep breath before continuing. "He's convinced me that counseling will help with my nightmares and flashbacks. Not overnight, of course. It'll take some time. But I've agreed to see him twice a week."

She wanted to shout *hallelujah*. "That's wonderful, Nick. I'm sure he'll be able to help you."

"Yeah, I hope so." His stance relaxed a little, and he ran the tip of his finger over the edge of the prep table. "Walker talked a lot psychological mumbo jumbo but the main idea is that he's going to help me remember what happened, think about it real hard, in a place where I feel safe. Like in his office."

"That sounds a little scary to me."

"He claims it'll get easier each time I go back there, to Afghanistan, in my head."

"I think it's very brave of you to try to get better."

"I don't know about brave, but I'm going to do it." A muscle jumped in his jaw and his Adam's apple bounced. "See, the thing is, I don't know how long it will take for me to get past my nightmares and flashbacks, but I want to stay here in Bear Lake. And someday, I want you to be my wife." His fingertips caressed her cheek, a light touch so moving that she felt it clear into her soul. "I love you, Alisa. I think I have since that day when I saw you swinging that big ol' ax. And I want to marry you."

"Oh, Nick…" Without hesitation, filled with joy,

she stepped into his arms, and he held her. His jacket was a little rough against her cheek, and he smelled of cleansing rain. She ran her fingers through his damp hair. "I love you, too. I didn't want to. I was afraid—"

"I know. Me too."

"Yes, I'll marry you. Today. Tomorrow. Whenever you're ready."

He lifted her chin, covering her mouth with his. His kiss transported her to a world she'd always dreamed of, a place filled with love and caring, a creation built on the foundation of marriage, family and faith.

When he broke the kiss, Nick was breathing hard. "There's one hitch." He brushed another kiss to her lips. "I'm not going to marry you until I can support you and Greg. I don't want anyone to think you've married a bum. So I'm going to be looking for a job."

A smile curved her lips. "I think there's a way we can fix that." She walked over to the linen cupboard and pulled out a white chef's coat. "Take off your jacket, soldier. It just so happens, the Pine Tree Diner has an opening for a chef. It seems Mama Machak is falling for Dr. McCandless. So we're going to need a hotshot chef to carry on."

"Sounds like a good deal to me. In fact, now that I think of it, I've got a little money stashed away. Haven't had a chance to spend much in the last few years."

"Oh?"

He slipped on the jacket she handed him. She smoothed it over his broad shoulders. "Very handsome, sir."

"Maybe you and Mama would let me buy into the diner, become a partner? Then we can work together to turn this into a real profit-making organization."

"I think us being partners in every way is sheer genius." Her heart overflowing with love and dreams of their future together, she stood on tiptoe to kiss him again. "Welcome home, soldier."

# *Epilogue*

On a spring day in Bear Lake in Pastor Walker's church office, Alisa smiled as Jolene, her matron of honor, zipped up her cream-colored wedding dress. The simple boat neckline and a calf-length skirt, in contrast to her usual slacks and sweater, made her feel like she was going to a dress-up party.

*Her wedding!* She could hardly believe the day had finally arrived.

Mama, looking beautiful in a violet dress, handed Alisa the bouquet of spring flowers she'd carry down the aisle. Mama had worked herself silly for the reception to be held in the diner banquet room. There were big pots of mushroom soup, trays of paprika chicken and dumplings, authentic goulash, side dishes of sauerkraut, creamed peas, carrot-and-apple salad and apple strudel for dessert waiting for the guests.

There was a knock on the door. Dr. McCandles

appeared and the sound of organ music drifted into the room.

"It's time for us to be seated, Ingrid."

Smiling, with just a trace of tears in her eyes, she kissed Alisa on the cheek. "Be happy, my little Alisova."

"I will be, I promise." So much joy filled her heart, she was sure it would last her a lifetime with Nick and beyond.

A few minutes later, Nick's friends Ned Turner and Ward Cummings arrived to escort Alisa and Jolene down the aisle.

Taking Ned's arm, Alisa walked with him to the back of the church and waited while Ward and Jolene made their way down the center aisle.

Ward whispered, "Nick's a lucky guy."

"So am I." Her gaze traveled to Nick, wearing a white dinner jacket, standing tall and strong beside the pastor. Sweetly, Nick asked Greg to be his best man. Rags, freshly bathed and wearing a bow tie for a collar, sat proudly at Greg's side.

Nick hadn't totally tamed the memories of that terrible day in Afghanistan, but he had found ways to accept that he had survived for a reason.

As the music changed, the congregation stood and Alisa took the first step toward the man she loved. She was sure the Lord had brought Nick home to her.

* * * * *

Dear Reader,

I hope you have enjoyed visiting one of my favorite places—the fictional town of Bear Lake, Montana, not far from Glacier National Park. The scenery is spectacular, the people friendly and the weather? Well, that depends on the day, as Nick, Alisa and Greg learned when they enjoyed a picnic on the far side of the lake.

Nick Carbini, the hero of this story, suffers from post-traumatic stress disorder (PTSD). According to a 2009 study by the think tank RAND Corporation, an estimated 20 percent of returning veterans, or 300,000 service members, have symptoms of PTSD or major depression. In 2012, the Veterans Administration acknowledged the problem by adding more counselors trained to treat PTSD.

It's not by accident that Rags, the stray dog Nick adopted, wakes him when he has a nightmare and calms him. Both the VA and the Army are conducting studies to determine if the anecdotal evidence that dogs help PTSD patients is valid. Several nonprofit groups are working to directly provide veterans with dogs, and Assistance Dogs International, which represents dog training organizations, conducts extensive training programs.

We owe our returning veterans more than we

can ever repay. I hope every one of them receives whatever treatment they need and a dog to love too.

Meanwhile, look for more of my books set in Bear Lake, Montana. It's a great place to visit.

Happy reading….

Charlotte Carter

## Questions for Discussion

1. Do you think it was right for Nick not to tell Alisa right away about his post-traumatic stress disorder (PTSD)?

2. What other traumatic event besides being in a war might cause someone to develop PTSD?

3. How do you feel about the developing relationship between Mama and Dr. McCandless?

4. How would you feel if your daughter fell in love with a man who had spent three years in prison?

5. Was it reasonable of Alisa to be so wary of all men after Ben deserted her when she was pregnant? Should she have been more open to developing a new romantic relationship?

6. Have you ever worked as a waitress? What was that experience like? Would you do it again?

7. Would you like to have a summer cabin on a lake? What lake activities would you enjoy?

8. Would you want to live in a tourist town? Why or why not?

9. What challenges does Alisa face raising a son on her own?
10. What is your favorite meal when you eat in a restaurant?
11. Is your pastor trained to counsel those who are suffering from PTSD? Are you or your friends close to anyone who has suffered with PTSD?
12. Is there a Veteran Affairs facility near you where veterans can go to get help?
13. Do you enjoy putting jigsaw puzzles together? How about crossword puzzles or sudoku?
14. Have you or a family member served in the military? What adjustments were required to make that service successful?
15. In Alisa's eyes, Nick was a hero. How do you define being heroic?